AHMADOU KOUROUMA

Allah Is Not Obliged

Ahmadou Kourouma (called "one of the major figures of contemporary African literature" by *Le Figaro*) was born in 1927 in the small town of Boundiali in the Ivory Coast. As a young man he fought in the French colonial army in Indochina and studied science in France. Returning to the Ivory Coast, Kourouma worked in insurance but did not stay there for long. He was jailed over ideological clashes with the government; subsequently he spent many years in exile.

Kourouma was a playwright and the author of four novels, of which *Allah Is Not Obliged* is the most recent and winner of the prestigious Prix Renaudot. *Waiting for the Wild Beasts to Vote* won the Prix du Livre Inter in 1999. Ahmadou Kourouma died in 2003.

ALSO BY AHMADOU KOUROUMA

Waiting for the Wild Beasts to Vote
Monnew
The Suns of Independence

Allah Is Not Obliged

Ahmadou Kourouma

TRANSLATED BY FRANK WYNNE

ANCHOR BOOKS

A DIVISION OF RANDOM HOUSE, INC.

NEW YORK

FIRST ANCHOR BOOKS EDITION, MAY 2007

Translation copyright © 2006 by Frank Wynne

All rights reserved. Published in the United States by Anchor Books,
a division of Random House, Inc., New York. Originally published in
France as *Allah n'est pas obligé* by Editions du Seuil, Paris, in 2000.
Copyright © 2000 by Editions du Seuil. This translation
originally published in the United Kingdom by
William Heinemann, London, in 2006.

Anchor Books and colophon are trademarks of Random House, Inc.

Library of Congress Cataloging-in-Publication Data:
Kourouma, Ahmadou.
[Allah n'est pas obligé. English]
Allah is not obliged / by Ahmadou Kourouma ;
translated by Frank Wynne.—1st Anchor Books ed.
p. cm.
ISBN 978-0-307-27957-6
I. Title.
PQ3989.2.K58A5513 2007
843'.914—dc22
2006037947

www.anchorbooks.com

Printed in the United States of America
10 9 8 7 6 5 4 3 2 1

To the children of Djibouti:
it is at your request that I write this book.

And to my wife, for her patience.

Translator's Note

In her speech at the 2003 PEN Tribute, the peerless translator Edith Grossman best explained the translator's task: 'Fidelity is our noble purpose, but it does not have much, if anything, to do with what is called literal meaning. A translation can be faithful to tone and intention, to meaning. It can rarely be faithful to words or syntax, for these are peculiar to specific languages and are not transferable.' Never have these precepts been as clear to me than in teasing out the poetry and the voices of Ahmadou Kourouma.

For help with the languages of West Africa, I am indebted to the Agence Intergouvernementale de la Francophonie and to Robert Perron for his concordance of Kourouma's locutions; for recordings of the oral narratives of child-soldiers, I am grateful to Tony Tate and Human Rights Watch; for a map through the political labyrinth of West Africa, I have had frequent recourse to nationmaster.com and sierraleone.org.

In his article 'Writing as Translation', Kwaku A. Gyasi writes: 'The translator of francophone African literature has to go beyond the French expression to the other culture, the other psychology that lies beneath it, that is, to reach the African context which is its focus.' When all else has failed, I have been guided by my ear, and by the music of contemporary *griots* Abdul Tee-Jay, Usifu Jalloh and Bajourou.

1

The full, final and completely complete title of my bullshit story is: *Allah is not obliged to be fair about all the things he does here on earth.* Okay. Right. I better start explaining some stuff.

First off, Number one . . . My name is Birahima and I'm a little nigger. Not 'cos I'm black and I'm a kid. I'm a little nigger because I can't talk French for shit. That's how things are. You might be a grown-up, or old, you might be Arab, or Chinese, or white, or Russian – or even American – if you talk bad French, it's called *parler petit nègre* – little nigger talking – so that makes you a little nigger too. That's the rules of French for you.

Number two . . . I didn't get very far at school; I gave up in my third year in primary school. I chucked it because everyone says education's not worth an old grandmother's

1

fart any more. (In Black Nigger African Native talk, when a thing isn't worth much we say it's not worth an old grandmother's fart, on account of how a fart from a fucked-up old granny doesn't hardly make any noise and it doesn't even smell really bad.) Education isn't worth a grandmother's fart any more, because nowadays even if you get a degree you've got no hope of becoming a nurse or a teacher in some fucked-up French-speaking banana republic. ('Banana republic' means it looks democratic, but really it's all corruption and vested interests.) But going to primary school for three years doesn't make you all autonomous and incredible. You know a bit, but not enough; you end up being what Black Nigger African Natives call grilled on both sides. You're not an indigenous savage any more like the rest of the Black Nigger African Natives 'cos you can understand the civilised blacks and the *toubabs* (a *toubab* is a white person) and work out what they're saying, except maybe English people and the American Blacks in Liberia, but you still don't know how to do geography or grammar or conjugation or long division or comprehension so you'll never get the easy money working as a civil servant in some fucked-up, crooked republic like Guinea, Côte d'Ivoire, etc., etc.

Number three . . . I'm disrespectful, I'm rude as a goat's beard and I swear like a bastard. I don't swear like the civilised Black Nigger African Natives in their nice suits, I don't say fuck! shit! bitch! I use Malinké swear words like *faforo!* (my father's cock − or your father's or somebody's father's), *gnamokodé!* (bastard), *walahé!* (I swear by Allah). Malinké is the name of the tribe I belong to. They're Black Nigger

African Savages and there's a lot of us in the north of Côte d'lvoire and in Guinea, and there's even Malinkés in other corrupt fucked-up banana republics like Gambia, Sierra Leone and up in Senegal.

Number four . . . I suppose I should apologise for talking right at you like this, on account of how I'm only a kid. I'm maybe ten, maybe twelve (two years ago, grandmother said I was eight, maman said I was ten) and I talk too much. Polite kids are supposed to listen, they don't sit under that talking-tree and they don't chatter like a mynah bird in a fig tree. Talking is for old men with big white beards. There's a proverb that says, 'For as long as there's a head on your shoulders, you don't put your headdress on your knee.' That's village customs for you. But I don't give two fucks about village customs any more, 'cos I've been in Liberia and killed lots of guys with an AK-47 (we called it a 'kalash') and got fucked-up on kanif and lots of hard drugs.

Number five . . . To make sure I tell you the life story of my fucked-up life in proper French, I've got four different dictionaries so I don't get confused with big words. First off, I've got the *Larousse* and the *Petit Robert*, then, second off, I've got the *Glossary of French Lexical Particularities in Black Africa*, and, third off, I've got the *Harrap's*. The dictionaries are for looking up big words and checking big words and particularly for explaining big words. I need to be able to explain stuff because I want all sorts of different people to read my bullshit: colonial *toubabs*, Black Nigger African Natives and anyone that can understand French. The *Larousse* and the *Petit Robert* are for looking up and checking and explaining

3

French words so I can explain them to Black Nigger African Natives. *The Glossary of French Lexical Particularities in Black Africa* is for explaining African words to the French *toubabs* from France. The *Harrap's* is for explaining pidgin words to French people who don't know shit about pidgin.

How did I get the dictionaries? That's a long story that I don't feel like going into right now. Because I haven't got time 'cos I don't want to get tied up in bullshit. That's why. *Faforo!*

Number six . . . Don't go thinking that I'm some cute kid, 'cos I'm not. I'm cursed because I did bad things to my maman. According to Black Nigger African Native customs, if your mother is angry with you and she dies with all that anger in her heart, then she curses you and you're cursed. And afterwards nothing ever goes right for you or anyone who knows you.

I'm not some cute kid on account of how I'm hunted by the *gnamas* of lots of people. (*Gnamas* is a complicated Black Nigger African Native word that I need to explain so French people can understand. According to the *Glossary*, a *gnama* is the shadow of a person that remains after death. The shadow becomes an immanent malevolent force which stalks anyone who has killed an innocent victim.) And I killed lots of innocent victims over in Liberia and Sierra Leone where I was a child doing tribal warfare, and where I got fucked-up on lots of hard drugs. The *gnamas* of the innocent people I killed are stalking me, so my whole life and everything round me is fucked. *Gnamokodé!*

So that's me – six points, no more no less, with my cheeky

4

foul-mouthed attitude thrown in for good treasure. (Actually, you don't say 'for good treasure', you say 'for good measure'. I need to explain 'for good measure' for Black Nigger African Natives who don't know nothing about anything. According to *Larousse*, it means extra, on top of everything else.)

So that's me, and it's not an edifying spectacle. Anyway, now that I've introduced myself, I'm really, truly going to tell you the life story of my cursed, fucked-up life.

Sit down and listen. And write everything down. *Allah is not obliged to be fair about everything he does. Faforo!*

Before I got to Liberia, I was a fearless, blameless kid. I slept anywhere I wanted and stole all kinds of stuff to eat. My grandmother used to spend days and days looking for me: that's because I was what they call a street kid. Before I was a street kid, I went at school. Before that, I was a *bilakoro* back in the village of Togobala (according to the *Glossary*, a *bilakoro* is an uncircumcised boy). I ran through the streams and down to the fields and I hunted mice and birds in the scrubland. I was a proper Black Nigger African Native Savage. Before that, I was a baby in maman's hut. I used to scamper between maman's hut and grandmother's hut. Before that, I crawled around in maman's hut. Before I was crawling around on all fours, I was in maman's belly. And before that, I could have been the wind, or maybe a snake, or maybe water. You're always something like a snake or a tree or an animal or a person before you get born. It's called life before life. I lived life before life. *Gnamokodé!*

The first thing inside me . . . In proper French, you don't

5

say 'inside me', you say 'in my mind'. Well, the first thing inside me or in my mind when I think about maman's hut is the fire, the glow of the embers, the flicker of flame. I don't know how many months old I was when I grilled my arm. Maman hadn't been counting my age, she hadn't got time on account of how she spent all the time suffering and crying.

I forgot to tell you something major, something really extremely important. Maman walked round on her arse. *Walahé!* On the two cheeks of her arse. She propped herself up on her hands and her left leg. Her left leg was as withered as a shepherd's crook and her right leg – the one she called her crushed serpent's head – was amputated and crippled by the ulcer. (According to my *Larousse*, an 'ulcer' is 'an inflammatory and often suppurating lesion on the skin or an internal mucous surface resulting in necrosis of tissue'). It's like a blister that never gets better and ends up killing you. Maman's ulcer was swathed in leaves wrapped up in an old *pagne* (a loin-cloth). Her right leg was permanently sticking up in the air. Maman moved on her arse like a caterpillar in fits and starts ('fits and starts' means 'stopping suddenly then starting again'). I was still crawling back then. I could tell you what happened, I can remember. But I don't like to tell everyone about it. Because it's a secret, because when I tell the story I tremble from the pain like I'm terrified on account of the fire searing in my skin. I was running around on all fours and maman was chasing me. I was going faster than she was. She was chasing after me, her right leg stuck up in the air, moving on her arse in fits and starts, leaning on her arms. I went too far, too fast, 'cos I was trying not to get

6

caught. I made a dash and fell on to the glowing embers. The fire did its job and grilled my arm. It grilled the arm of a poor little kid because Allah doesn't have to be fair about everything he does here on earth. I still have the scar, on my arm, in my head, in my belly like the Black Africans say, and in my heart. It's still there in my heart, in my whole being, like the smell of my mother. My body is saturated with maman's nauseating smell. (According to the *Larousse*, 'nauseating' means 'capable of arousing aversion or disgust' and 'saturated' means 'drenched or soaked with liquid'.) *Gnamokodé!*

Anyway, even back when I was a cute kid, back in my childhood, there was this ulcer eating into maman's right leg and rotting it. An ulcer that steered my mother (to 'steer' is 'to guide someone somewhere'). An ulcer that steered my mother and the rest of the family. And, around my mother and her ulcer was the hearth. The hearth that grilled my arm. The hearth always belching smoke or sparks; it spits sparks when you poke the fire to get it going. All round the hearth there were *kanaris* (according to the *Glossary*, a *kanaris* is a handcrafted earthenware jar). There were *kanaris* and more *kanaris*, and every one of them filled with decoctions (that means liquid obtained from the action of boiling plants). The decoctions were used for flushing maman's ulcer. There were more *kanaris* lined up along the wall at the back of the hut. Between the *kanaris* and the hearth, there was my mother and her ulcer wrapped up in a *pagne*. There was me, and there was the marabout, hunter and healer, Balla. Balla was maman's healer.

Balla was a great guy and totally extraordinary. He knew all these countries and other stuff. Allah had given him hundreds of incredible destinies, and talents and opportunities. He was a freedman – according to *Larousse*, that's what they called someone who used to be a slave but is now free. And he was a *donson ba*, that's the name we give to a master huntsman who has killed black game and at least one malevolent djinn, according to the *Glossary*. Balla was a kaffir – that's what you call someone who refuses to believe in Islam and keeps his grigris. (According to the *Glossary*, a 'grigri' is 'a protective amulet, often a piece of paper inscribed with magical incantation kept in a small leather purse which is tied above the elbow or around the neck'.) Balla refused to burn his false idols, so he wasn't a Muslim, he didn't perform the five daily prayers, or fast for one month every year. The day he dies, no Muslim is allowed to go to his funeral, and they're not allowed to bury his body in the Muslim cemetery. And strictly speaking, nobody's allowed to eat the meat of any animal whose throat he slits.

Balla was the only Bambara ('Bambara' means 'one who refuses'), the only kaffir, in the village. Everyone was afraid of him. He had grigris round his neck and all over his arms, in his hair and his pockets. No one in the village was allowed near Balla's hut, but actually at night everyone went to his hut. Some people even went during the day, because Balla practised sorcery, native medicine, magic and a million other extravagant customs ('extravagant' means 'unrestrained or recklessly wasteful').

All the stuff I bullshit about ('bullshit' means 'to say stupid

8

things'), I learned from Balla. A man should always thank the shea tree for the fruits gathered from beneath its branches. I will always be grateful to Balla. *Faforo! Gnamokodé!*

There were two doors to maman's hut: the big door that opened on to the family concession and the little door on to the yard. (According to the *Glossary*, a 'concession' is an enclosed piece of land often used for business.) I was crawling around all over the place and getting into everything. Sometimes, I'd fall on to maman's ulcer and she'd howl with the pain. The ulcer would start bleeding. Maman would howl like a hyena with its paws caught in the teeth of a wolf trap. She would start crying. Maman had too many tears, the corners of her eyes were always full of tears and her throat was always full of sobs suffocating her.

'Dry your tears and stop your bawling,' grandmother used to say. 'Allah created each one of us and decided our fate, the colour of our eyes, our height and our sufferings. You were born with pain from your ulcer. It is He who gave you your time to live out on this earth in a hut, wrapped in a blanket near a hearth. You should pray *Allahu Akbar! Allahu Akbar!* (Allah is great!) Allah does not mete out suffering without cause. He makes you suffer here on earth to purify you so that one day he can grant you paradise and eternal happiness.'

Mum dried her tears and stopped crying and we'd go back to playing our games and chasing each other round the house. Then there was one morning when she stopped playing with me, howling in pain and choking from her sobs.

'I don't know what you're whining about. You should pray *Allahu Akbar! Allahu Akbar!* You should give thanks to Allah for his goodness. Here on earth, he has struck you down with a suffering whose days are numbered. Suffering a thousand times less terrible than the fires of hell. The fires of hell that the evil, the damned and the wicked will suffer for all eternity.'

Grandmother said this and asked maman to pray. Maman dried her tears and prayed with grandmother.

The day my arm got grilled, maman cried and cried and her throat and her chest were all swollen with sobs. My grandmother and father showed up and they both lost their temper and yelled at maman.

'This is simply another ordeal which Allah has sent you (an 'ordeal' is 'a severe or trying experience intended to judge someone's worth'). If Allah has ordained that you be miserable here on earth, it is because he has reserved some greater happiness for you in paradise.'

My maman dried her eyes, swallowed her sobs and prayed with grandmother. Then maman and I went back to playing chase.

Balla used to say no kid ever leaves his mother's hut because her farts stink. Maman's smells never bothered me. The hut was full of all kinds of stink. Farts, shit, piss, the infected ulcer, the bitter smoke, and the smells of Balla the healer. But I didn't even smell them, so they didn't make me puke. Maman's stink and Balla's stink smelled good to me. I was used to them. It was surrounded by these smells that I ate and slept best. It's called a natural habitat and every animal has one; maman's hut with her smells was my natural habitat.

I think it's a pity we don't know how the world was before we get born. Sometimes, I'd spend the morning trying to imagine what maman was like before her circumcision, the way she sang and danced and walked when she was a young virgin before her excision. Grandmother and Balla always said she was pretty as a gazelle, pretty as a *gouro* mask. I only ever got to see her lying down or crawling around on her arse, I never saw her standing, but I knew she must have been charming and beautiful, because even after thirty years of shit and stink, of smoke from the hearth and suffering and tears, there was still something beautiful about the lines on her face. When the lines on her face weren't brimming with tears, her face shone with a kind of glow. A bit like a lost blemished pearl, ('blemished' means 'marked by imperfections'). Her beauty was decaying like the ulcer on her leg, but the glow just shone right though the smoke and the smells of the hut. *Faforo! Walahé!*

When maman was pretty and charming and virginal, people used to call her Bafitini. Even now when her body was all fucked-up and rotting, Balla and grandmother still called her Bafitini. I'd only ever seen her at her worst, in the last stages of her multifarious, multicoloured decay, but I called her *Ma*. Just Ma. African people would say it came from deep in my insides; French people in France would say it came from my heart.

Grandmother says maman was born in Siguiri, one of the

hundreds of shit-holes in Guinea, Côte d'Ivoire and Sierra Leone where miners and rock-breakers dig for gold. Grandfather was a big gold trader. Like all the other filthy rich traffickers, he bought himself lots of women and horses and cows and big starched *bubus* (a *bubu* is a long tunic worn by Black Nigger African Natives). The women had lots of babies and the cows had lots of calves. Grandfather needed somewhere to put all the women and the kids and the cows and the calves and all his gold, so he bought lots of houses and lots of concessions, and when he couldn't buy more, he built more. Grandfather had concessions in every settlement where there were fortune-hunting gold miners.

Grandmother was my grandfather's first wife and maman was one of his first children, that's why he sent grandmother to the town to look after the family business. He didn't want her hanging around some mining outpost full of bandits and cut-throats and liars and gold dealers.

Besides grandmother had to stay in town so maman didn't die of her heart stopping dead or the ulcer rotting her completely. Maman used to say she'd drop dead from the pain if grandmother left her to go out to the gold-mining camps where grandfather did his business and where there were cut-throats lying in wait for women.

Grandmother really loved my mother, but she didn't know what date she was born, or even what the day of the week it was. She was far too busy that night, the night my mother was born. Balla says it doesn't matter what date you're born, or what day of the week you're born, seeing as how everyone has to get born some day or other, somewhere or other, and

12

everyone has to die some day or other, somewhere or other, so we can all be buried in the same clay and rejoin our ancestors and discover the ultimate judgement of Allah.

On the night maman was born, grandmother was far too busy on account of the bad omens that were happening all over the universe. There were lots and lots of bad omens in heaven and on earth that night — hyenas howling in the mountains, owls crying on the roofs of the huts. The omens signified that maman would have a life that was tremendously and catastrophically catastrophic. A life of shit and suffering and damnation, etc.

Balla said he and grandmother offered up sacrifices but they weren't enough to undo maman's terrible fate. Allah doesn't have to accept sacrifices and neither do the spirits of the ancestors. Allah can do whatever he feels like; he doesn't have to acquiesce to every prayer from every lowly human being ('acquiesce' means 'agree to'). The spirits of the ancestors can do what they like; they don't have to acquiesce to all our complicated prayers.

Grandmother loved me. Me, Birahima. She treasured me. She loved me more than her all her other grandchildren. If anyone gave her a lump of sugar or a ripe mango or a papaya or some milk, she would save them for me and no one else. She wouldn't eat a single bit. She'd hide whatever they gave her in a corner of the hut so she could give it to me when I got home sweating, tired, thirsty, starving like a real street urchin.

When maman was young and a virgin and pretty as a jewel, she used to live in the mining camp where my grandfather did his gold business. The place was crawling with cut-throats and gold dealers going round raping uncircumcised girls and slitting their throats. That's why maman didn't stay there. At the very first harmattan ('harmattan' means 'a season marked by hot dry easterly winds', according to the *Glossary*), she was sent back to Togobala for the ceremony of excision, where girls are initiated every year when the north wind blows.

No one in Togobala knows where in the savannah the excision will be performed until it happens. At cockcrow, the girls come out of their huts and in single file ('single file' means 'one after the other in a line'), they walk in silence into the forest. They get to the place of excision just as the sun appears. You don't have to have been to the place of excision to know they cut something out of the girls. They cut something out of my mother, but unfortunately maman's blood didn't stop, it kept gushing like a river swollen by a storm. All her friends had stopped bleeding. That meant that maman was the one who was to die at the place of excision. That's the way of the world, the price that has to be paid. Every year at the ceremony of excision, the djinn of the forest takes one of the girls who has come to be initiated and kills her and keeps her for a sacrifice. The girl is buried there in the forest. The djinn never chooses an ugly girl, it always picks one of the most beautiful, one of the prettiest of the girls to be initiated. Maman was the prettiest girl of her age, that was why the djinn chose her to die in the forest.

The sorceress who was the excisor was one of the Bambara (an 'excisor' is a woman who performs female circumcision).

14

In our country, the Horodougou, there are two peoples, the Bambaras and the Malinkés. People from families like Kourouma, Cissoko, Diarra, Konaté are Malinkés, we're Dioulas and Muslims. The Malinkés aren't from here; they came from the valley of the Niger long, long ago. The Malinkés are good people who heed the word of Allah. They perform the five daily prayers, they don't drink palm wine or eat pork or any game killed by kaffir *obayifos* like Balla (an *obayifo* is a shaman or a grigriman). All the other villages are Bambaras, pagans, kaffirs, unbelievers, animists, savages, shamans. Sometimes the Bambaras are called different things like Lobis or Sénoufos or Kabiès. Before people came to colonise them, they didn't wear any clothes. They were called the naked peoples. Bambaras are true indigenes, the true ancient owners of the land. The woman who was performing the excision was a Bambara named Moussokoroni. When Moussokoroni saw my mother lying there bleeding and dying, she took pity on her because maman was still really beautiful back then. Lots of kaffirs who know nothing of Allah are completely evil, but some kaffirs are good. Moussokoroni had a good heart and worked her magic and she was able to rescue maman from the clutches of the murderous evil spirit of the forest. The spirit accepted Moussokoroni's prayers and the sacrifices and maman stopped bleeding. She was saved. My grandfather and my grandmother were happy and so was everyone from the village of Togobala and they wanted to give the sorceress a reward and pay her lots of money; but Moussokoroni refused. She refused to take their reward.

Moussokoroni did not want money or cattle or cola nuts

or millet or palm wine or clothes or cowries (a cowrie is a type of shell that originally comes from the Indian ocean which plays an important role in traditional life, mostly as a kind of money). Moussokoroni thought maman was beautiful, so beautiful that she wanted my mother to be her son's wife.

Her son was a hunter, a kaffir, a shaman, a pagan animist. A pious Muslim girl who reads the Qur'an like my mother is not allowed to marry a kaffir. The whole village refused.

My mother married my father on account of how he was her cousin and the son of the village imam. So Moussokoroni, who was a shaman, and her son, who was also a shaman, got really, really angry. They cast spells on my mother's right leg, an evil spell called a *koroté* (a venom that acts on the victim from a distance, according to the *Glossary*) and a really powerful *djibo* (which is an evil curse).

After maman was married and was in her confinement on account of being pregnant, a black dot, a tiny black dot, appeared on her right leg. Maman was in pain from the small black spot so they lanced it, they made a small cut to lance the spot and put medicine on the cut. But the cut didn't heal – it started to gobble up maman's foot, to gobble up her leg.

Straight away, my father and my grandmother went to see Balla, they consulted grigrimen and marabouts and shamans and everyone said that maman didn't get better because of the *koroté*, the evil spell that Moussokoroni and her son had cast. They went to the village where Moussokoroni and her son lived but it was too late.

Moussokoroni was already dead, good and dead from old

16

age and good and buried too. Her son, the hunter, was an evil man; he refused to listen, refused to understand, refused to confess. He was completely evil, a genuine kaffir, an enemy of Allah.

Maman gave birth to my big sister. By the time my sister was walking and talking and going to school the abscess was still eating away at maman's leg, so she was taken to the district hospital. This was long before independence. At the hospital, there was a white doctor – a *toubab* – with three stripes on his shoulder, a black doctor with no stripes, a male nurse who was a major, a midwife and a bunch of other black people wearing white coats. All the black people in white coats were civil servants who were paid by the colonial government. Back then, if you wanted a civil servant to treat you properly, you had to bring them a chicken. That's the custom in Africa. Maman gave chickens to five different civil servants and they all treated maman properly and took good care of her, but even with all the bandages and the permanganate, her ulcer still didn't get better, it just kept bleeding and rotting. The *toubab* doctor said they were going to have to amputate maman's leg, cut it off at the knee and throw the rotten bit out for the dogs at the rubbish tip. But luckily one of maman's chickens had gone to the nurse who was also a major and he came in the middle of the night to warn her.

The nurse said that what maman was suffering from was not a *toubab* disease, it was a Black Nigger African Native disease. A disease that the medicine and the science of the white man could not cure. 'Only the grigris of an African healer can heal your wound. If the captain operates on your leg, you will die, absolutely die, you will die like a dog,' said the nurse who was also a major. The nurse was a Muslim and could not tell a lie.

Grandfather hired a donkey driver. In the middle of the night, by moonlight, the donkey driver and Balla the healer went to the hospital and kidnapped maman like a pair of bandits. Before dawn, they took her deep into the forest where they hid her under a tree in a dense thicket. The *toubab* doctor was furious and came to the village in his military uniform and had his guards surround the village. They searched for maman in every single hut but they didn't find her, because no one in the village knew where in the forest she was hidden.

After the captain and the guards left, Balla the healer and the donkey driver went into the forest and brought maman home where she went back to moving around on her arse in fits and starts. *Faforo!*

Now, everyone was convinced that maman had a Black Nigger African native disease that couldn't be cured by *toubab* doctors, it could only be cured by the native remedies of a shamanic healer. So the villagers collected some cola nuts, and took two chickens – one white and one black – and a cow, to take as sacrificial offerings to Moussokoroni's son who had helped cast the evil spell, the *koroté*, on my mother's leg because he was jealous that he couldn't marry her. They were going to ask the kaffir for mercy, ask him to rescind the *djibo*, the curse. Everything had been prepared.

Then, early one morning, they were surprised when three old men from Moussokoroni's village suddenly showed up, three genuine old kaffir shamans wearing filthy *bubus* – as filthy and disgusting as a hyena's anus. They had been chewing cola nuts for so long that two of them were, as toothless as a chimpanzee's arse. The third kaffir was almost toothless as well, except for two green teeth on his bottom jaw for grigris. They had chewed tobacco for so long that their beards were as red as the rat in maman's hut, not white like the beards of old Muslim men who perform the five daily prayers. They walked slowly, hunched over their sticks like snails. They had brought cola nuts, two chickens – one black and one white – and a cow. They had come to ask for mercy, because Moussokoroni's son, the evil kaffir hunter, was dead. He had tried to shoot an evil spirit in the form of a buffalo deep in the deep forest. The buffalo had run him through with its horns, lifting his body off the ground and then throwing him down and trampling him completely to death with his intestines and his insides all mashed up in the mud.

The death had been so terrible, so strange, that the villagers consulted grigrimen and marabouts and shamans and everyone said that the evil djinn in the form of a buffalo was an avatar of my mother Bafitini (an 'avatar' is the manifestation of a spirit in human or animal form). What they meant was that it was my mother's spirit that had changed itself into the buffalo. It was maman's spirit that had killed Moussokoroni and her son by devouring their souls (according to the *Glossary*, a devourer of souls is one who kills by consuming the life-force of his victim). It meant they believed that my mother was the most powerful sorceress in the whole country: that her magic was stronger than the magic of Moussokoroni and her son. She was the leader of the soul-eaters and all the sorcerers in the village and every night she and the other sorcerers would devour souls and she would even devour her own ulcer. That was why the ulcer never healed. No one in the world could ever heal her ulcer because every night my mother devoured souls and devoured her own rotting leg, so it was her own fault that she had to move around on her arse in fits and starts with her right leg permanently stuck up in the air. *Walahé!*

When I found out about all this stuff, when I found out that my mother was a devourer of souls and was even devouring her own rotting leg, I was so astonished, so sickened, that I cried. I cried and cried all day and all night for four days. On the morning of the fifth day, I left maman's hut forever and decided that I was never going to eat with maman ever again. That's how disgusting I thought she was.

That's when I became a street kid. A proper street kid that sleeps with the goats, and nicks stuff to eat from fields and concessions.

Balla and grandmother found me living rough and brought me back. They dried my tears and tried to placate me ('placate' means they tried to calm my feelings of anger and hurt), they said that maman wasn't a witch, that she *couldn't* be a witch, because she was a good Muslim. They said the Bambara kaffirs were barefaced liars.

What Balla and grandmother said didn't really convince me, it was too late. Once a fart is out of your arse you can't put it back. I was still a bit suspicious of maman, with misgivings and qualms in my belly, like Africans say, or in my heart, like French people say. I was scared she'd devour my soul. When someone devours your soul, you can't keep on living so you die of a disease or an accident. You die some kind of terrible death. *Gnamokodé!*

When maman died, Balla said that it wasn't because her soul had been devoured. He knew because he was a marabout who knew all about sorcery, a *feticheur* with the power to detect soul-eaters. My grandmother explained that maman had been killed by Allah with just the ulcer and all the tears she was always crying. Because Allah up in heaven can do whatever he likes; he doesn't have to be fair about what he does here on earth.

That was when I realised that I'd hurt my mother, hurt her really badly. Hurt someone who was crippled. She never said anything to me about it but she died with all the hurt in her heart, and now I was cursed and damned and I'd never do any good here on earth. I'd never be worth anything to anyone on this earth.

I might tell about maman's death some other time. But I don't have to and you can't make me. *Faforo!*

I haven't told you anything about my father yet. He was called Mory. I don't really like talking about my father. It makes me sad in my heart and in my belly. On account of how he died without ever growing a wise old man's white beard. I don't talk about him very often because I never really knew him. I never really spent any time with him on account of how he died while I was still crawling around on all fours.

21

Balla the healer was the person I spent all my time with, he was the person I loved. Fortunately, Balla the *feticheur* knows lots of things. He knows magic and he's travelled all over the place hunting in Côte d'Ivoire, in Senegal, even in Ghana and Liberia where the black people are Black Americans and where the indigenes speak pidgin. Over there, that's what they call English.

Issa is my uncle, that's what your father's brother is called. After my father died, my mother belonged to Issa, and he was supposed to marry her. That's the tradition of the Malinké tribe.

But no one in the village wanted to hand my mother over to Issa because he never came to see maman in her hut and never looked after me, and he was always saying cruel things about my father and my grandmother and even my grandfather. Everybody thought that the tradition didn't count. And anyway Issa didn't want a wife who walked around on her arse with her rotting leg stuck up in the air.

According to the laws of the Qur'an and of religion, maman was not allowed to stay unmarried for more than a year of twelve moons, she had to be properly married with a proper dowry of cola nuts. (According to the *Glossary* a cola nut is the seed of the cola tree eaten for its stimulating properties. Cola nuts are ritual gifts in traditional societies.) Maman had to say something, she had to decide, she had to choose.

Maman told grandmother that Balla was the only person who came to her hut day and night, and she wanted to have a marriage with a proper cola nut dowry with her healer and *feticheur* Balla. When everyone heard, they howled and they yapped like a pack of mad dogs, they were all dead set against the marriage because Balla was a Bambara kaffir who didn't perform the five daily prayers and didn't fast during Ramadan, so he couldn't be allowed to marry a devout Muslim like my mother who performed her five daily prayers religiously every day.

There were speeches, and readings from the Qur'an, but in the end maman and Balla went to see the imam – that's what you call the old man with the white beard who stands up in front of everyone on Fridays and holy days and prays and sometimes even does it five times a day. The imam told Balla to repeat '*Allahu Akbar* and *bismillah*' over and over. Balla only said '*Allahu Akbar* and *bismillah*' once and after that everyone was happy for maman to have her marriage with the proper cola nut dowry with Balla.

That's how Balla got to be my stepfather. That's what your mother's second husband is called. Balla and maman had a *mariage en blanc*.

Even if the man and woman getting married are black, and they both wear black clothes, if they never do sex together then it's a white marriage – a *mariage en blanc* in French. It had to be a *mariage en blanc* for two reasons. First because Balla had all his grigris round his neck and down his arms and round his belt and he refused to undress in front of a woman. And second, because even if he took off all his grigris, he would never have been able to make babies with maman. On account of he didn't know my father's technique. My father hadn't had time to teach Balla the proper gymnastic way to wrap himself around maman so he could insert the

23

babies, seeing as how maman walked on her arse with one leg stuck up in the air on account of her ulcer.

My dad, he made three babies with my mother. My sister Mariam, my sister Fatouma, and me. My father was an important farmer and a devout believer who always made sure that maman had enough to eat. Grandmother said my father died in spite of all the good deeds he did on earth, because no one can know the will of Allah and because the Almighty up in heaven doesn't give a shit and does whatever he wants, and he doesn't have to be fair about everything he decides to do here on earth.

My maman died because Allah wanted her back. The imam said that a devout Muslim isn't allowed to criticise Allah or say anything bad about him. Then he said that my mother didn't die of magic, she died of her ulcer. Her leg just kept on eating away at her because after Moussokoroni and her son died there was no one left who could heal it on account of it wasn't a disease that could be cured in a *toubab* hospital. And because the time Allah had accorded her on earth was up.

Then the imam said that what the filthy old kaffirs had said was not true. He said it wasn't true that maman used to magically eat away at her rotting ulcer at night. But it didn't placate me and I started crying for my mum all over again. Then the imam said that I had not been kind to maman. In the village, the imam is the marabout with the big white beard who stands up on Fridays at one o'clock and leads the big prayer. So now I was really starting to feel sorry for what I'd done.

Even now, it hurts, it burns my heart every time I think about maman's death because I think maybe maman really wasn't a witch who devoured souls and that makes me remember the night she died.

When maman started to rot away, to really rot away, she sent for me and squeezed my left arm really hard with her right hand. I couldn't escape and run away and be a street kid that night so I slept in the blanket with her and maman's soul left her body at the first cockcrow. In the morning, maman's fingers were holding on to my arm so tight that Balla and my grandmother and another woman had to use all their strength to drag me away from my mother. *Walahé!* That's the truth.

Everyone cried and cried on account of how maman had suffered so much down here on earth. They all said maman would go straight up to heaven to be with Allah because of all the hardships and sufferings she'd had down here on earth and because Allah didn't have any more hardships and sufferings left to give her.

The imam said that her spirit would be a good spirit, a spirit that would protect the living against troubles and evil spells, a spirit that should be worshipped and commemorated. Now maman is in heaven and she's not suffering any more, so everyone down here on earth is happy. Except me.

Maman's death makes me sad, even now it makes me sad. Because the accusations that the old kaffir men said were just lies, they were barefaced liars. And I had been a horrible, cruel son to her. I hurt maman, and she died with that hurt in her heart. That's why I'm cursed and the curse goes with me wherever I go. *Gnamokodé!*

* * *

For my mother's funeral, on the seventh and fortieth days my aunt Mahan came from Liberia. (According to the *Glossary*, the seventh and fortieth days are the days on which ceremonies are held to the memory of the deceased.)

Mahan is the mother of Mamadou. That's why Mamadou is my cousin. My aunt Mahan lived in Liberia, deep in the forests, far, far away from any road. She ran away to Liberia with her second husband because her first husband, Mamadou's father, was a master huntsman. A master huntsman who yelled at her and cursed her and threatened her with knives and guns. He was what they call a bully. Mamadou's father, the master huntsman, was a big bully. My aunt had made two babies, my cousin Férima and my cousin Mamadou, with the master huntsman. The name of the master huntsman, Mamadou's father, was Morifing. But Morifing cursed and punched and threatened my aunt so much that one day she left him and ran away.

Everywhere in the world a woman isn't supposed to leave her husband's bed even if that husband curses her and punches her and threatens her. The woman is always wrong. That's what they call women's rights.

It wasn't independence yet. My aunt was summoned to the office of the *toubab* commissioner in charge of the district. On account of women's rights, the two children were taken from their mother and given to their father. To make sure that my aunt didn't steal her children, to make sure she didn't even see them, their father sent them to Côte d'Ivoire. He sent my cousin Mamadou to his uncle who was an important nurse. The nurse sent Mamadou to the white school in Côte d'Ivoire.

In those days there weren't too many schools, so education was still worth something. That's how Mamadou was able to grow up to be a big somebody, even a doctor.

Even though she got a divorce from the colonial *toubab* commissioner on account of women's rights, and even though Morifing got to keep the two children, the evil huntsman was always trying to find my aunt and her second husband. Sometimes, in the night, he'd wake all alone and fire his rifle into the air and scream how he was going to kill them and hunt them down like deer if he ever set eyes on them. So my aunt and her second husband went far away from French colonies like Guinea and Côte d'Ivoire to hide in the forests of Liberia, because it is a colony full of American blacks where they don't apply the French rules about women's rights. Because the English they speak there is called pidgin. *Faforo!*

The evil huntsman was not in the village for my mother's funeral, because every year he left for months and months to go far away to different countries where he was still a bully and still hunted lots of wild animals to sell their meat. That was his work, his job. It was only because he was far away that my aunt came to the village to help us, grandmother, Balla and me, to mourn for my mother.

Three weeks after my aunt came to the village, there was a big family palaver in grandfather's hut. ('Palaver' means 'a traditional assembly where outstanding issues are discussed and decisions are made.') At the palaver there was my grandfather, my grandmother, my aunt and a whole bunch of other aunts and uncles. They decided, according to the laws of Malinké families, that because my mother was dead, my aunt would be my second mother. A second mother is also called a tutor. My aunt – my tutor – had to feed me and clothe me and she was the only person who was allowed to insult me and punish me and make sure I got a proper education.

Everyone decided that I should go to Liberia to live with my aunt, because here in Togobala I never went to the French school or even to the Qur'anic school. I was always skipping classes to be a street kid or to go hunting in the forests with Balla, who was teaching me hunting and animism and magic instead of teaching me the holy word of Allah from the Qur'an. My grandmother didn't approve of what Balla was teaching me. She wanted to send me away, far away from Balla, because she was afraid I would grow up to be a Bambara kaffir *feticheur*, and not a proper Malinké who performs the five daily prayers.

Grandmother tried to encourage me, to persuade me to leave Balla, by telling me that in my aunt's house in Liberia I would have rice and meat with *sauce graine* to eat. I was happy to be leaving because I wanted to eat lots of rice with *sauce graine. Walahé!*

But the council of the elders told my grandmother and my grandfather that I was not allowed to leave the village because I was still a *bilakoro*. (*Bilakoro* is what you call a boy who hasn't been circumcised and initiated yet.) You see, it's different in Liberia, there's lots of forests and the people that live there are called bushmen. (According to the *Glossary*, 'bushmen' means 'men of the forests – an offensive name given to forest dwellers by the peoples of the savannah'.) Bushmen are people of the forests who aren't Malinkés and who don't know about circumcision and initiation. So the council said I had to stay until the dry season, when I was part of the first group of *bilakoros* to be prepared for circumcision and initiation.

One night, someone came and woke me, and we walked and walked and at dawn we all arrived at a clearing on the edge of the jungle at the place of circumcision. You don't have to have been to the place of circumcision to know that they cut something off. All the *bilakoros* dug a little hole and sat in front of it. The man who was performing the circumcisions came out of the forest carrying as many limes as there were *bilakoros*. He was very tall and very old and he looked like a blacksmith. He was also a powerful *feticheur* and a mighty shaman. With every lime he cut, a boy's foreskin fell. He came to me and I closed my eyes and my foreskin fell into the hole. It's really painful, but that's the Malinké tradition.

All the boys slept near the village in a camp deep in the dense thicket where we lived for two months.

During those two months, they taught us things, lots of things that we were obliged never to reveal to anyone ever. That's why it's called initiation. I would never talk to anyone who was not initiated about the things I learned during initiation. On the day we left the sacred forest, we ate a lot and danced a lot, and we weren't *bilakoros* any more: we had been initiated so now we were men. Now I was allowed to leave the village and nobody could object or complain.

So there we were, my aunt, who was my second mother or tutor, and me, Birahima, a fearless and blameless boy, both ready to leave for Liberia when suddenly, one night, as the fourth prayer was being said, we heard shouting and gunfire coming from my aunt's first husband's hut. Everyone in the village was yelling that the bully huntsman was back. My aunt was terrified, she didn't stop for a second, she disappeared into the night, right into the forest without me. It was only two weeks later, when we knew my aunt had arrived back safely to her husband in Liberia, that my grandmother and the elders of the village started looking for someone who could go with me to my aunt's house in Liberia.

In our tribe, everyone knows the names of the people from our village who are now big-shots with lots of money in Abidjan, Dakar, Bamako, Conakry, Paris, New York, Rome; some of them are even living in countries far across the Ocean where it's always cold like America and France. A person who gets to be a big somebody is also called a hajji, because every year they go to Mecca and over there in the desert they slit a sheep's throat during the big Muslim feast called *la fête des moutons* that is also called *el-kabeir*.

That's why everyone in the village knows about Yacouba. Yacouba is from Togoballa but now he was a big somebody in Abidjan and did the big hajj there in his big starched *bubu*.

One morning I woke up and everyone in the village was saying that Yacouba had come back during the night. But they all had to keep quiet and not say anything about Yacouba being back. They all knew that the man who had arrived back in the village was really called Yacouba, but now they had to forget the name Yacouba and call him Tiécoura instead. Every day, five times a day, they saw him going to the mosque but no one was allowed to tell anyone else that they had seen Yacouba-alias-Tiécoura with their own two eyes (when someone has one name but you're supposed to call them by a different name it's called 'alias'). Yacouba-alias-Tiécoura had been in the village for two moons and nobody called him Yacouba any more and nobody even asked why a big somebody like him had come back to the village.

Since they couldn't find anyone in the village to take me to my aunt's house in Liberia, one morning after prayer Yacouba-alias-Tiécoura, the big somebody hajji said he would take me to Liberia. He said he wanted to go with me because he was also a money multiplier. A money multiplier is a marabout that you give a little handful of money to one day and another day he gives you back a big fistful of CFA francs or even American dollars. Tiécoura was a money multiplier, but he was a marabout fortune-teller too and a marabout who made grigris.

Tiécoura was in a hurry to get away because everybody said that, with all the tribal wars and everything in Liberia, marabout money multipliers and shamans and healers and grigri makers could make lots of money and even American dollars. They earned a lot of money in Liberia because there was nobody left except the rebel warlords and people who were too scared to die. A warlord is a big-shot who's killed lots of people and has his own country with villages full of people that he's allowed to kill anytime he likes for no reason. With all the rebel warlords and all their people, Tiécoura knew he would be able to do business there with no trouble from the police like he got in Abidjan. He was always in trouble with the police for all the work and all the business he did in Abidjan, Yopougon, Port-Bouët and different villages in Côte d'Ivoire like Daloa, Bassam, Bouaké and even Boundiali in *Sénofou* country up in the north.

Yacouba-alias-Tiécoura was a real big big-shot, a genuine hajji. When he was circumcised, he left the village to sell cola nuts all over the bushmen villages in the forests of Côte d'Ivoire like Agloville, Daloa, Gagnoa or Anyama. In Anyama he got rich by shipping lots and lots of baskets of cola nuts to Dakar by boat. By wetting beards (that means bribing people, also known as paying *baksheesh*), by wetting the beards of the customs officers, Yacouba's cola nuts got on the boat in Abidjan and off the boat in Dakar without paying a penny in taxes or duties. If someone tries to export cola nuts and doesn't bribe the customs officers in Senegal and Côte d'Ivoire, they have to pay lots of import taxes and duties like government levies and they don't make a penny for themselves. Yacouba's cola nuts — which he never paid a penny tax on — were sold off to the highest bidder in Senegal with loads of profits. With all the profits, Yacouba-alias-Tiécoura got rich.

As soon as he was good and rich he took the plane and

went to Mecca so he could be a hajji, and the minute he was a hajji he came back to Abidjan to marry lots of women. To be able to marry lots of women, he bought lots of concessions and businesses in Anyama and other godforsaken holes in Abidjan, like Abobo. Once he'd bought the concessions, he had a lots of empty houses and empty space, so all his parents and his friends, and his parents' friends and his friends' friends, and his wives' parents came to stay in the rooms to get well fed and have lots of palavers. Whenever he wasn't praying, Yacouba-alias-Tiécoura sat under an appatam all day listening to all the palavers (an 'appatam' is a small building on stilts with a roof of thatched palm leaves which serves as shelter from the sun). He'd spend all day discussing stuff under the appatam in his big starched *bubu* and saying lots of big-turbaned hajji proverbs and suras from the Qur'an.

This one month, he was so busy listening to the palavers and dealing with all the shit from the palaverers that he completely forgot to remember to wet the beards of the customs officers for a boatload of cola nuts, but it got shipped anyway and arrived in Dakar.

In Dakar, the dock workers were on strike and the dockers and the customs officers just left the cola nuts to rot away on the boat while Yacouba-alias-Tiécoura went on blethering under the appatam. The whole boatload of baskets of cola nuts was completely fucked, completely ruined, they were only good for chucking into the sea, and Yacouba lost all the money he had. In French, when that happens, you'd say that Yacouba was ruined and totally bankrupt.

When you're ruined and bankrupt, the people from the

bank come and ask you to give them back all their money, the money that they were kind enough to lend you, and if you don't pay them back them immediately, they take you to court. Then, you have to wet the beards of the magistrates and judges and stenographers and lawyers in the courts at Abidjan, because if you don't they find you completely guilty. If they find you guilty, you have to wet the beards of the bailiffs and the police, because if you don't they seize all your stuff and all your houses.

The bailiffs and the police seized all Yacouba-alias-Tiécoura's property and he ran away to Ghana so as he didn't have to watch them take all his things and so they didn't get their hands on his wives' jewellery.

Ghana is one of the countries near Côte d'Ivoire where they're really good at football and where people speak pidgin instead of English.

In Ghana, there was lots of merchandise, and everything was a lot cheaper than it was in Abidjan. By wetting the beards of the customs officers at the border, Yacouba shipped the merchandise into Côte d'Ivoire without paying any taxes and sold all the stuff to the highest bidder with lots of profits. With all the profits, he got rich and bought a big property in Yopougon Port-Bouët where he had lots of wives and turbans and starched *bubus* and fast getaway cars for to drive people in a hurry. Lots and lots of fast cars.

When Yacouba-alias-Tiécoura found out one of his drivers was skimming the profits, he got in the car himself and went to add up all the receipts, but the driver who was driving was angry and pissed off and had a fatal accident. Yacouba was badly hurt and put in hospital, but Allah made him better because Yacouba performs the five daily prayers every day and was always slitting the throats of sacrifices. Allah made him better because his sacrifices were fitting. (Among Black Nigger African Natives, if you say 'the sacrifices were fitting', it means you got lucky.)

Yacouba got two things out of the accident and being in hospital. Firstly, number one, he got a limp and people started calling him the crippled crook. Secondly, number two, he got the idea that Allah never leaves empty a mouth he has created. *Faforo!*

While Yacouba-alias-Tiécoura was in hospital, one of his friends went to visit him. The friend's name was Sekou, Sekou Doumbouya. He was the same generation as Yacouba and they were friends from when they got initiated, so they'd been friends a long time. (In Black Nigger African Native villages, all the kids are grouped by age group and everyone always does everything with their own group. They all play together and get initiated together.) Sekou came to visit in a Mercedes Benz. Sekou told Yacouba about his business, which earned him lots and lots of money and he didn't have to do fuck all. Sekou worked as a marabout. When he got out of the CHU hospital in Yopougon, Yacouba-alias-Tiécoura sold his car and all his other fast cars and set himself up as a marabout money multiplier maker of grigris and inventor of sayings and prayers to help people find out what sacrifices to make so they can defend themselves against evil spells.

It was a good job for him, because lots of ministers and deputies and high-up civil servants and rich people and big-shots all started coming to his house. And when all the bad guys and the cut-throats and the other murderers in Côte d'Ivoire saw what was happening, they started going round to Yacouba's house with big suitcases full of stolen money asking him to multiply the money they got from all the robbing.

In Abidjan, when the cops see a bad guy with a gun in his hand, they don't stop and chat, they shoot him quick like a deer or a rabbit and ask questions later. One day, the police shot three bad guys. Two of them died right away, but before the third guy died, he told the police that all their stolen money was with the money multiplier Yacouba-alias-Tiécoura, so the police went straight round to the money multiplier's house.

Maybe it was because he made fitting sacrifices (according to the *Glossary*, 'fitting' means 'auspicious or favourable' – Black Nigger African Natives make lots and lots of bloody sacrifices, and when they are fitting that means Allah is favourable), maybe it was his fitting sacrifices or maybe he was just lucky, but when the police came straight round and searched his house and found lots and lots of suitcases full of stolen money Yacouba-alias-Tiécoura wasn't home.

Yacouba never went back home. He left Abidjan in the middle of the night and aliased his name to Tiécoura and spent all his time hiding in Togobala where everybody who saw him said they hadn't seen him. Yacouba still believed, and even said out loud, Allah never leaves empty a mouth he has created.

This is the guy who was supposed to go with me to my aunt's house in Liberia. *Walahé!* It's the truth.

One morning, he came to see me and took me aside and secretly told me things in confidence. He told me Liberia was a wonderful country and that over there his job money multiplying was like gold. Over in Liberia they called him a grigriman. A grigriman is a big somebody over there. He told me lots of other stuff about Liberia to convince me to go with him. *Faforo!*

Wonderful things. He said they had tribal wars in Liberia, and street kids like me could be child-soldiers, which is pidgin and according to my *Harrap's* in American they call them small-soldiers. Small-soldiers had every-fucking-thing. They had AK-47s. AK-47s are Kalashnikov guns invented by the Russians so you can shoot and keep shooting and never stop. With the AK-47s the small-soldiers got every-fucking-thing. They had money, they even had American dollars. They had shoes and stripes and radios and helmets and even cars that they call four-by-fours. I shouted *Walahé! Walahé!* I want to go to Liberia. Right now this minute. I want to be a child-soldier, a small-soldier. Child-soldier and small-soldier is *kif-kif*, that means it's the same difference. In bed, when I did pooh-pooh or pee-pee, I shouted out small-soldier, child-soldier, soldier-child!

One morning at first cockcrow, Yacouba came to our hut. It was still dark; grandmother woke me up and gave me rice and peanut sauce. I ate a lot. Grandmother came with us, and when we got to the edge of the village where the rubbish tip is, she put a silver coin in my hand that was probably all the savings she had. Even today I can still feel how warm the silver coin felt in the palm of my hand. Then she cried and went back to the hut. I'd never see her again. That's how Allah wanted it. And Allah isn't fair about all the stuff he does here on earth.

Yacouba told me to walk ahead of him. Yacouba had a limp, that's why they called him the crippled crook. Before we left, he told me that we would never go hungry on our journey, because Allah in his infinite goodness never leaves empty a mouth he has created. With our bags on our heads, we set off on foot before dawn, Tiécoura and me, for the market town where there are trucks that will take you to other capital cities in Guinea, Liberia, Côte d'Ivoire and Mali.

We didn't get far, not even a whole kilometre, because suddenly an owl gave a terrible cry on our left and flew out of the grass and disappeared into the dark. I jumped I was so scared and I screamed 'Maman!' and clung to Tiécoura's legs. Tiécoura, who was a fearless and blameless man, recited one of the biggest, most powerful suras he knows off by heart. After that, he said that when an owl flies past a traveller from left to right it's a really bad portent for the journey (a 'portent' is something that predicts the future). He sat down and recited three more big important suras from the Qur'an and three really scary native shaman prayers. Automatically, a touraco started singing somewhere on our right ('touraco': a large fruit-eating bird, according to the *Glossary*). Once the touraco had sung on the right, Yacouba got up and said that the touraco singing was a good omen. A good omen meant we were protected by my maman's spirit. Maman's spirit is really powerful on account of all the crying and suffering she did here on earth. Maman's spirit cleared our path of the ill-omened cry of the owl ('ill-omened' means that something bad, maybe even death, is coming). Even though I was cursed by my mum, her spirit was protecting me.

On we went, foot to the road (according to the *Glossary*, 'foot to the road' means 'walking') and not saying anything because we were feeling all strong and confident.

We didn't get far, foot to the road, not even five kilometres when suddenly another owl gave a terrible cry in the grass and disappeared into the dark. I was so really, totally scared that I screamed 'Maman!' twice. Yacouba-alias-Tiécoura who is a fearless and blameless man when it comes to magic and sorcery and stuff recited two of the most powerful suras that he knows off by heart. Then he told me that when two owls fly up from the left in front of a traveller, it's a really bad, totally bad augury (an 'augury' is something that seems to predict the future). He sat down and said six big important suras from the Qur'an and six big shaman prayers. Automatically, a partridge sang on our right and Yacouba stood up and he smiled and said that the partridge singing meant that we were protected by my maman's spirit. Maman's spirit is really good and really powerful on account of all the crying and walking round on her arse she did here on earth. Maman's spirit cleared the path in front of us of the ill-omened cry of the second owl. Maman was really good, she was protecting me even though I really, really hurt her.

And we kept on walking, foot to the road, with no worries because we were really happy and proud.

We didn't get far, foot to the road, not even ten kilometres: suddenly on the left a third owl gave a terrible cry in the grass and flew off into the dark. I was so really, totally, absolutely scared that I screamed 'Mum!' three times. Tiécoura who is a fearless and blameless man when it comes to magic and sorcery recited three of the most extremely powerful suras that he knows off by heart. Then he said that when three owls fly up from the left in front of a traveller it's a three-times terrible omen for the journey. He sat down and recited nine more big important suras from the Qur'an and nine big shaman prayers. Automatically, a guineafowl sang on our right and Yacouba stood up and smiled and said that the guineafowl singing meant that we were blessed by maman's spirit. Maman's spirit is too good and too powerful on account of all the crying and walking round on her arse she did here on earth. My mum's spirit had cleared the path of the ill-omened cry of the third owl. And we kept on walking, foot to the road, not thinking too much because we were so happy and relieved.

Morning started to rise and we kept on walking. Suddenly all the birds on earth, in the trees, in the sky, started singing because they were all so happy. That made the sun come out, and it jumped up right in front of us, up above the trees. We were happy too. We were looking at the top of the kapok tree of the next village far away when suddenly we saw an eagle fly up on our left. The eagle was really heavy because it had something in its claws. When it got as far as us, the eagle dropped whatever it was carrying on to the path. It was a dead hare. Tiécoura shouted lots of *bismillahs* and prayed for a long time, a really long time, and said lots of suras and kaffir animist prayers. He was really, really worried and said that the dead hare in the middle of the path was a really bad, totally bad augury.

When we arrived, we didn't go to the truck station straight away because we got to the village wanting to give up and go back to Togobala on account of how there had been so many bad omens.

But then we saw an old, worn-out grandmother leaning on a long stick and Yacouba gave her a cola nut and she was happy and said we should go and talk to some man who had just arrived in the village. This man was the most powerful marabout, medium and grigriman in the village and the whole district (a 'medium' is someone who is reputed to have the ability to communicate with spirits). We walked past three concessions and two huts and came slap bang on the marabout's place. We waited in the vestibule, seeing as how there were other people ahead of us. When we walked into the hut, surprise! The marabout was Sekou himself, Yacouba's friend from his initiation who came to see him in the Mercedes when he was in Yopougon hospital in Abidjan. Yacouba and Sekou hugged. Sekou had been forced to leave Yacouba and abandon his Mercedes and all his merchandise on account of some murky business to do with money multiplying (according to the *Petit Robert*, 'murky business' means 'a deplorable or lamentable affair'). As soon as we sat down in the hut, Sekou, using prestidigitation, made a white chicken appear from his sleeve. Yacouba gasped in amazement.

Me, I was terrified. Sekou advised us to do lots of sacrifices, really big sacrifices, so we sacrificed two sheep and two chickens in a graveyard, the chicken he pulled out of his sleeve and another one.

The sacrifices were fitting. Allah and the spirits of the ancestors didn't have to accept them; they accepted the sacrifices because they wanted to. We were relieved. Sekou also advised us not to leave until Friday. He said that, for travellers who had seen a dead hare in their path, Friday was the only day he would counsel ('counsel' means 'strongly advise'). Because Friday is the holy day of the Muslims, of the dead, and even of grigrimen.

We were optimistic and strong because Allah in his infinite goodness never leaves a mouth he has created without subsistence ('subsistence' means 'food or means of survival'). This was in June 1993.

Before I forget, I should say that when we were talking Yacouba persuaded Sekou to come to Liberia and Sierra Leone with us, because in those countries the people were dying like flies, and when people are dying like flies a marabout who can pull a chicken out of his sleeve can make piles of money and heaps of dollars. He didn't say no. And actually, we met him a couple of times in the inhospitable jungles of Liberia and Sierra Leone.

That's all I've got to say for today. I'm fed up talking, so I'm going to stop.

Walahé! Faforo! Gnamokodé!

2

When people say there's tribal wars in a country, it means that big important warlords have divided the country up. They've divided up all the money, all the land, all the people. They divide up everything and the whole world lets them, everyone in the whole world lets them kill innocent men and children and women. And that's not all! The funniest thing is that the warlords are all using desperate measures to hang on to all the things they've got, but the same warlords are doing everything they can to get their hands on more stuff (according to the *Larousse*, 'desperate measures' means 'all-out physical force').

In Liberia, there were four big important warlords: Doe, Taylor, Johnson and the Hajji Koroma, as well as a bunch of small warlords. The small warlords were doing their best to be big warlords. And everything in the whole country had been divided up. That's why they say there was tribal wars in Liberia. And that's where I was going. And that's where my aunt lived! *Walahé!* It's the truth!

In tribal wars and even in Liberia, the child-soldiers, the small-soldiers, don't get paid. They just kill people and steal everything worth stealing. In tribal wars and even in Liberia, the soldiers don't get paid. They massacre the people and keep everything worth keeping. So as they have enough to eat and all the other stuff they need, the child-soldiers and the real soldiers sell off everything they steal really cheap.

That's why in Liberia you can get everything really cheap. You can get cheap gold, cheap diamonds, cheap TVs, cheap four-by-fours, cheap guns and AK-47s or kalashes. Every, every fucking thing is cheap.

And when everything in a country is cheap, dealers flock to that country (according to *Larousse*, 'flock' means 'to arrive in great numbers'). Dealers who want to get rich quick all go to Liberia to buy and exchange things. They go with a fistful of rice, a tiny bit of soap, a bottle of petrol, a couple of dollars or even a few CFA francs, because everybody needs them and nobody's got them. They sell the stuff they bring or trade it for cheap merchandise and bring the cheap merchandise back to Guinea or Côte d'Ivoire and sell it to the highest bidder. That's how you make big money.

It's on account of all the big money that you see hundreds of men and women in N'Zérékoré swarming round the *gbakas* leaving for Liberia. ('*Gbaka*' is a Black Nigger African Native word. You can find it in the *Glossary of French Lexical Particularities in Black Africa*, and it means a car or a vehicle.)

And whenever a country is doing tribal wars, everyone travels in convoys. (A convoy is when you've got lots of *gbakas* travelling together.) Everyone came to Liberia in convoys. There's motorbikes up front and at the back of the convoy. On the motorbikes there are men armed to the teeth ready to defend the convoy, because as well as the four big important warlords, there are lots of small important warlords who do road blocks and stick-ups (according to my *Larousse*, a 'stick-up' is when you take by force something which is not legally yours).

So we go to Liberia in a convoy and to make sure we don't get in a stick-up, we have a motorbike riding up front and that's how we set off. *Faforo!*

There he was, this little guy, in pidgin they say a kid (according to my *Harrap's*, 'kid' means 'a boy or young man'). Anyway there was this little guy standing right slap bang exactly at a turn in the road and the motorbike that was supposed to be protecting us didn't manage to stop dead when this little kid signals to stop. The two guys on the motorbike thought it was a road-block so they opened fire and there's this kid, this child-soldier, lying there, fucked. Dead, totally dead. *Walahé! Faforo!*

There was a second, a minute, of silence before the storm. And then the whole forest all around us started spitting, the *tat-tat-tat tat-tat-tat tat-tat-tat* of AK-47s. So when the *tat-tat-tat* of the kalashes started up, the birds in the forest could tell something wasn't right, so they all took off and flew away towards more peaceful skies. The AK-47 *tat-tat-tat* sprays all over the motorbike and the guys on the motorbike, the driver and the other guy who was all *faro* on the back with his own kalash. ('*Faro*' isn't in the *Petit Robert*, but it's in the *Glossary* and it means 'showing off'.) So now the driver and the guy acting all *faro* were both dead. Absolutely, one hundred percent dead. But there's still AK-47s going *tat-tat-tat*-ing! *tat-tat-tat*-ing! And you could already see all the destruction all over the road – the burning motorbike and bodies all AK-47ed and all the blood, lots and lots of blood, the blood just never got tired of flowing. *Faforo!* All this just kept happening and happening, the sinister *tat-tat-tat* music kept going ('Sinister' means 'serious, scary, terrifying').

Let's start from the start.

Mostly, things don't happen like that. Mostly, the bike or the car or whatever stops dead when the kid makes the signal and doesn't go past him even one inch. When it happens like that, everything goes smoothly, very smoothly. *Faforo!* The kid, the child-soldier, who's about as tall as an officer's cane, chats to the guys on the motorbike protecting the convoy. They get to know each other a bit, laughing and joking as if they drank beer together every night. Then the kid whistles, then he whistles again. Then a four-by-four truck comes out of the forest all covered in camouflage leaves. A four-by-four full of kids, child-soldiers, small-soldiers. Kids about this tall . . . as tall as an officer's cane. Child-soldiers showing off, their kalashes, their AK-47s, slung over their shoulders, all dressed in Para uniforms. All dressed in parachute gear way too big for them, so the uniforms are falling down round their knees, and they're swimming in them. The funniest thing is that there's girls, genuine girls with real AK-47s showing off. But there aren't too many girls. Only the cruel ones: only the one's who'd stick a live bee right in your eye. (When someone is really cruel, Black Nigger African Natives say 'they'd stick a live bee right in your eye'.) Then you'd see lots more child-soldiers dressed in the same uniforms, with the same guns, but walking out of the forest, or hanging off the cars and chatting to the people in the convoy like they were best friends who did their initiation together. (In the village, doing your initiation together means you're really good friends.) Then the four-by-four truck drives to the front of the convoy and they all head off together.

Then, you arrive in a camp that belongs to Colonel Papa le Bon. Everyone in the convoy gets out and goes into Colonel Papa le Bon's hut. They unpack everything, weigh everything, measure everything on account of the taxes and duties are based on how much all the stuff is worth. There's a lot of palaver and arguing and after a while you reach an agreement. Then you pay and pay and pay. You pay in kind, with rice, manioc, *fonio* ('*fonio*' is a food also called *acha*, or 'hungry rice'). You can even pay with American dollars, real American dollars. Then Colonel Papa le Bon organises an ecumenical mass. (In my *Larousse*, it says 'ecumenical' means a mass where there's Jesus Christ and Mohammed and Buddha.) So anyway, Colonel Papa le Bon organises an ecumenical mass. There's lots of blessings and stuff. Then he goes his way and you go your way.

That's the way it's supposed to happen. Because Colonel

Papa le Bon is the representative spokesman of the NPFL (which stands for National Patriotic Front of Liberia). The NPFL is the movement of the warlord Taylor, who wreaks havoc all over the region.

But that's not how things went with us. The guys at the front on the motorbike who were supposed to defend us thought the kid was a road-block and opened fire. And that's when the shit hit the fan.

All we could hear was the *tat-tat-tat* of AK-47s, just machine-guns *tat-tat-tat*-ing away. Whoever it was just kept shooting and shooting and shooting. When the damage was done, totally done, that's when it stopped.

While all this was going on, all of us in the convoy were going crazy. Everyone was screaming out to the spirits of their ancestors and to every protective spirit in heaven and on earth. With all the noise, it sounded like thunder. And all this because the guy on the motorcycle had been showing off with his kalash and fired at the child-soldier.

Yacouba had a bad feeling the minute we boarded the truck. He never liked the look of the guy on the back of the motor-bike, the one who fired the first shot, the one who thought the kid was just a little thief setting up a road-block. It was the guy on the back of the motorcycle who fired and made all the consequences happen and now we were in the shit.

Then we saw a child-soldier, a small-soldier as tall as an officer's cane, a child-soldier wearing a baggy Para uniform. It was a girl. She was walking hesitantly. ('Hesitantly' is what you say when someone is walking like they're nervous and

48

unsure.) And she looked round at all the destruction from the AK-47ing, looked really carefully as if one of the guys might get up when actually everyone was totally dead, even the blood was dead beat, from flowing all over the place. She stopped where she was and whistled loudly and then whistled again. And then child-soldiers started appearing from all over the place, all dressed like her, all waving their AK-47s.

First they surrounded us and started yelling, 'Out of the trucks, hands on your heads!' And we all started getting down, hands on our heads.

The child-soldiers were really, really angry; they were red in the face they were so angry. (You don't really say 'red in the face' for blacks. Blacks never go red in the face, they just frown.) Anyway the small-soldiers were frowning; they were crying on account of how angry they were, they were crying for their dead friend.

We started getting out of the trucks. Single file, one after the other. One of the soldiers took the jewellery, ripping off earrings and necklaces and stuffing them in a bag that another guy was carrying. The child-soldiers took our headdresses and clothes and shoes. If they liked your underwear, they took that too. They put all the clothes into piles, lots of piles: one pile for the shoes, one pile for the headdresses, one for pants, one for underpants. All the naked passengers from the trucks uncomfortably tried to cover their *bangala* if it was a man or their *gnoussou-gnoussou* if it was a woman (according to the *Glossary*, '*bangala*' and '*gnoussou-gnoussou*' are names for your shameful parts), but the child-soldiers didn't let them. They ordered the embarrassed passengers to fuck off into the forest. And everyone ran off into the forest with no objections.

When it came to Yacouba's turn, he wasn't going to be pushed around. He cried, 'Me marabout, me grigriman, me grigriman!'

The child-soldiers poked him and forced him to take off his clothes. He kept on shouting, 'Me shaman, grigriman. Me grigriman . . .' Even when he had no clothes on and was trying to cover his *bangala* with his hands, he kept on screaming, 'Grigriman, shaman.' And when they told him to go into the jungle, he came back shouting, 'Grigriman, shaman.' *'Makou!'* ordered the child-soldiers aiming an AK-47 at his arse. (*'Makou'* is in the *Glossary* and it means 'shut up'.) So he shut up and stood on the side of the road with his hands covering his shameful parts.

Then came my turn. I let them pull me to my feet. I was blubbering like a spoiled brat, 'Child-soldier, small-soldier, soldier-child, I want to be a child-soldier, I want to go to my aunt's house in Niangbo.' They kept taking my clothes off and I kept blubbering and crying, 'Me small-soldier, me child-soldier, me soldier-child.' Then they ordered me into the jungle but I wouldn't go, I just stood there with my *bangala* hanging there. I don't give a shit about modesty, I'm a street kid. (According to the *Petit Robert*, 'modesty' means 'a respect for moral standards'.) I don't give a fuck about moral standards, I just kept on crying.

One of the child-soldiers poked a kalash in my arse and shouted, *'Makou, makou!'* So I shut up. I was trembling, trembling like the hindquarters of a nanny-goat waiting for a billy-goat ('hindquarters' means 'arse, bum'). I felt like I needed to do pee-pee, to do pooh, to do everything. *Walahé!*

Next came a woman, a mother. She got down from the truck with her baby in her arms. A stray bullet had put a hole in the poor baby and killed it. The mother wasn't going to let herself be pushed around: she refused to take off her clothes. They tore off her *pagne* (according to the *Glossary*, a '*pagne*' is an item of traditional female clothing consisting of a piece of cloth without fastenings wrapped around the body). She refused to run into the forest, she stood beside me and Yacouba, on the side of the road, holding her dead baby in her arms. She started crying, 'My baby, my baby. *Walahé! Walahé!*' When I heard her, I started crying like the spoiled brat again, 'I want to go to Niangbo, I want to be a child-soldier. *Faforo! Walahé! Gnamokodé!*'

The concert got too deafening, too loud, and they finally started to pay attention. 'Shut the fuck up!' they ordered, and we went *makou*. 'Don't move!' and we stood to attention by the side of the road, like a bunch of fuckwits.

And then a four-by-four came out of the jungle. It was full of child-soldiers. They didn't wait for a signal, they just started looting the trucks. They took everything worth taking. They piled all the stuff into the four-by-four. The four-by-four made a couple of trips to the village. After they took all the things in the convoy, they started taking the piles of shoes and clothes and hats. They piled everything into the four-by-four and did another couple of trips. On the last run, the four-by-four brought back Colonel Papa le Bon.

*   *   *

Walahé! Colonel Papa le Bon was shockingly garbed (according to my *Larousse*, 'garbed' means 'dressed strangely'). For a start Colonel Papa le Bon had colonel's stripes. That was on account of the tribal wars. Colonel Papa le Bon was wearing a white soutane, a white soutane tied at the waist with a leather belt, a belt held up by a pair of black leather braces crossed across his back and his chest. Colonel Papa le Bon was wearing a cardinal's mitre. Colonel Papa le Bon was leaning on a pope's staff, a staff with a crucifix at the top. Colonel Papa le Bon was carrying a bible in his left hand. To top it all off, Colonel Papa le Bon was wearing an AK-47 slung over his shoulder. The AK-47 and Colonel Papa le Bon were inseparable, he carried it round with him night and day. That was on account of the tribal wars.

Colonel Papa le Bon stepped out of the four-by-four, he was crying. It's the truth, he was crying like a baby. He went over and crouched over the body of the child-soldier, the body of the little boy who had tried to stop the convoy. He prayed, then prayed some more. Then Colonel Papa le Bon came towards us. Wearing all the strange stuff he was wearing.

I started to cry again, 'I want to be a soldier-child, small-soldier, child-soldier, I want my auntie, I want my auntie in Niangbo!' A child-soldier with a machine-gun tried to make me swallow my sobs, but Colonel Papa le Bon stopped the kid and came over and patted my head like a proper father. I was happy and proud as a Senegalese wrestling champion. I stopped crying. With all his majesty, Colonel Papa le Bon gave a signal. A signal that meant they were going to take me with them. They gave me a *pagne* and I wrapped it round my arse and tied it.

Colonel Papa le Bon went over to Yacouba who started chanting again, 'I am a grigriman, I am a shaman.' The colonel made another signal and they brought Yacouba a *pagne* so he could hide his shameful parts. His *bangala* had shrunk.

Then Colonel Papa le Bon went over to the mother, the mother with the dead baby. He looked at her and looked at her. She was all filthy and she wasn't wearing her *pagne* any more and her underwear didn't really cover her *gnoussou-gnoussou*. She had a sensual charm, she had a voluptuous sex-appeal, ('sex appeal' meaning that she made you want to make love). Colonel Papa le Bon wanted to walk away, but he came back. He came back because the woman had voluptuous sex-appeal, he came back and stroked the baby. He ordered his people to come and take the baby.

They came with a makeshift stretcher and took the baby. (You say a 'makeshift stretcher' when the stretcher has been made in a hurry. That's what it says in the *Petit Robert*.) The dead bodies of the baby and the little boy were lifted on to the four-by-four on makeshift stretchers.

Colonel Papa le Bon climbed into the four-by-four. Four child-soldiers with AK-47s got into the car beside Colonel Papa le Bon. The truck set off. Everyone else followed, foot to the road. That's right, foot to the road. (I already explained 'foot to the road' means walking.)

We followed them. We means Yacouba, the mother of the dead baby, and your servant, me, the street kid, in the flesh. The truck headed towards the village slowly and silently.

Slowly and silently because it had dead people in it. That's what you do in everyday life, when you've got dead people on board, you drive slowly and silently. We were optimistic because Allah in his infinite goodness never leaves empty a mouth he has created. *Faforo!*

Suddenly Colonel Papa le Bon stopped the truck. He got out of the truck, everyone got out of the truck. Colonel Papa le Bon roared, a song that was powerful and melodious. The song was returned by the echo. The echo of the forest. It was the song of the dead in Gio. Gio is the language of the Black Nigger African Natives in these parts, it's a patois. Malinkés call them bushmen, savages, cannibals on account of they don't speak Malinké like us and they're not Muslim like us. In our big *bubus* the Malinkés look like they're kind and friendly but really we're racist bastards.

The song was taken up by the child-soldiers with the AK-47s. It was so, so beautiful that it made me cry. I cried my eyes out like this was the first time I'd ever seen something terrible. Cried like I didn't believe in Allah. You should have seen it. *Faforo!*

Everyone in the village came out of the huts. Out of curiosity, to see what was happening. The villagers followed the four-by-four with the bodies in it. Out of habit and because people are stupid and always following things. It was a genuine procession.

The dead child-soldier was called Kid, Captain Kid. Now and again in his beautiful song, Colonel Papa le Bon chanted 'Captain Kid' and the whole cortege howled after him

'Kid, Kid'. You should have heard it. They sounded like a bunch of retards.

We got to the camp. Like all the camps in the Liberian tribal wars, there were human skulls on stakes all round the boundary. Colonel Papa le Bon pointed his AK-47 in the air and fired. All the child-soldiers stopped dead and fired into the air like him. It was like I was dreaming. You should have seen it. *Gnamokodé!*

Kid's body was laid out under the appatam ('appatam' is in the *Glossary*, I explained it already).

Crowds and crowds came past every single second, all of them bending over the body and acting all sad as if people didn't go round slaughtering lots of innocents and children every day in Liberia.

That night, the funeral vigil started at nine o'clock after the Muslim prayers and the Catholic prayers. Nobody knew Kid's religion, on account of no one knew if his parents were Catholic or Muslim. It's *kif-kif*, same difference. The whole village was there for the vigil. There were lots of storm lanterns. It was spellbinding. ('Spellbinding' is a big word I found in the *Larousse*, it means something that is magical.)

Two women started a chant and then the choir and everyone else joined in. Once in a while, so as not to fall asleep, and so as not to be eaten alive by mosquitoes, they'd get up and shake their elephant tails. Because the women had elephant tails and they danced in a lewd way! In fact, it wasn't lewd, it was demonic. (According to the *Petit Robert*, 'lewd' means 'indecent or obscene'.)

Suddenly we heard a cry from some unfathomable depth.

The cry announced that Colonel Papa le Bon had joined the dance, that the master of ceremonies had entered the circle. Everyone stood up and took off their headdresses because he was the boss and the lord of the whole place. And we saw Colonel Papa le Bon completely transformed. Totally! *Walahé!* No shit!

He was wearing a multicoloured headwrap and he was stripped to the waist. He had muscles like a bull and it made me happy to see such a strong well-fed man in famine-starved Liberia. He had a bunch of medals hanging round his neck, from his arms and from his shoulders and in the middle of all the medals was his kalash. He had the kalash on account of there were tribal wars in Liberia and people were being killed like they weren't worth an old grandmother's fart. (In my village, when something's not worth much, we say it's not worth an old grandmother's fart. I explained that before and now I've explained it again.) Colonel Papa le Bon walked round the body three times then came and sat down. Everyone sat down and listened like a bunch of arseholes.

He started off by telling the events of how Captain Kid got killed. The two young men on the motorbike were possessed by evil spirits and fired on him without warning. The devil had got into them. The captain's soul flew off and we shall mourn him. We could not exorcise the devil from the hearts of every passenger in the convoy or from the minds of the men responsible for the captain's death. It just was not possible. That's why we had to kill some of them, but seeing as God says thou shalt not kill too much, or at least thou shalt kill less, we stopped killing, and left the others just as they came into the world. We left them naked. This is what the Lord has said: when people truly injure you, kill less but leave them naked they came into the world. Everything in the trucks and all their possessions were brought here to the camp. These things should be given to the captain's parents, but since no one knows who the captain's parents are, they will be distributed, shared out fairly between the child-soldiers, between Captain Kid's friends. The child-soldiers can sell off these things and make a couple of dollars. With the dollars they can buy lots of hashish. God will punish the people who committed the evil deed that killed Captain Kid.

Next, Colonel Papa le Bon told us what had to be done. *Walahé!* The devourer of souls had to be exposed. The devourer of souls who had gobbled up the child-soldier, Captain Kid, *djoko-djoko*. (According to the *Glossary*, '*djoko-djoko*' means 'by fair means or foul'.) He had to be hunted down in whatever form he had taken. There would be dancing all night and if necessary all the next day. The dance would go on until the devourer of souls had been unmasked. Until he had made a clean breast. (According to the *Larousse*, 'make a clean breast' means when someone confesses his terrible crime from his own lips.)

So as to look more serious and more approachable, Colonel Papa le Bon took off his kalash. He put the kalash close at hand, put it within easy reach on account of there was war and people were dying like flies from tribal wars in Liberia.

The tom-toms started up again, more furious, more hectic. And there were songs that were better than any nightingale's.

From time to time, palm wine was served, from time to time Colonel Papa le Bon drank palm wine, from time to time Colonel Papa le Bon got fucked-up on palm wine. But palm wine was not good for Colonel Papa le Bon. Not a bit. He drank the stuff all night, drank so much he was completely drunk and completely blacked out ('blacked out' means he became unconscious).

At about four in the morning, completely drunk, Colonel Papa le Bon staggered towards the circle of women and grabbed some old woman who was half-asleep. She had devoured the soul of Captain Kid! No one else! It was she. *Walahé!* She and nobody else who had been the leader of this debauchery. (According to my *Larousse*, 'debauchery' means 'an orgy'.)

The old woman shrieked like a bird in a trap, 'It wasn't me, it wasn't me!'

'It was you, it was you,' shouted Colonel Papa le Bon. 'The soul of Captain Kid has come back in the night to denounce you.'

'*Walahé!* It wasn't me. I loved Kid. He came to my hut to eat.'

'That's why you gobbled him up. I saw you transform yourself into an owl in the night. I was sleeping like a caiman, one eye half-open. I saw you. You took his soul in your claws. You flew up into the high branches of the kapok tree. Others transformed into owls flew up to join you. There you had your orgy. You gorged on his skull. You ate his brain yourself and left the remains to your disciples. It was you! It was you! It was you!'

'No, it wasn't me!'

'The soul of the dead came to me in the night to tell me it was you. If you don't confess, I will submit you to trial with a white-hot iron ('white-hot' means 'an object which has been subjected to heat until it glows'). I will pass the iron over your tongue. Yes, Yes.'

Faced with all the mounting evidence, the old woman was *makou*, open-mouthed. And then she told the truth, she made a clean breast, she confessed. ('Confess' is in my *Larousse*. It means to say in your own words that the incriminating facts are true.)

The old woman who confessed was called Jeanne. She and three of her disciples were taken to prison under escort. There, Colonel Papa le Bon was going to exorcise them ('exorcise' means 'to free from evil spirits or malign influences'). *Walahé! Faforo!*

Captain Kid's funeral took place then the next day at 4 p.m. It was raining. There was lots of crying. People were thrashing about and sobbing 'Kid! Kid! Kid!' like it was the first time they had ever seen a tragedy. And then the child-soldiers lined up and fired their kalashes. That's all they're good at. Firing guns. *Faforo!*

Colonel Papa le Bon was the representative of the NPFL in Zorzor. That was the highest up you could get in northern Liberia. It meant you looked after the important trafficking coming in from Guinea. You collected the taxes and customs duties and kept an eye on comings and goings in Liberia.

Walahé! Colonel Papa le Bon was a big-shot in the NPFL. An important member of Taylor's brigade.

Who was this big-shot warlord Taylor?

The first time anyone in Liberia heard of Taylor was when he pulled off a big gangster scam that bankrupted the Liberian treasury. He took all their money and used forged papers that he wrote himself to convince the government that he'd turned the money into loads of dollars in the USA. When they smelled a rat ('smelled a rat' means they realised there was something wrong) and discovered it was all a rip-off, they hunted him down. Taylor went into hiding in the USA using a false name. After a huge manhunt they tracked him down and arrested him. They put him in jail.

While he was locked up, he bribed his gaolers with stolen money and escaped to Libya, where he introduced himself to Qaddafi as the fearless leader of the revolution against Samuel Doe's bloody dictatorship. Qaddafi, the Libyan dictator, had been trying to overthrow Doe's regime and kissed Taylor right on the mouth. He sent them – Taylor and his followers – to the camps they have in Libya where they make terrorists. Libya has had terrorist camps ever since Qaddafi came to power. In this camp, Taylor and his followers learned guerrilla warfare.

And that's not all: Qaddafi palmed him off on Blaise Compaoré, the dictator of Burkina Faso, with lots of commendations, like he was commendable. Compaoré, the dictator of Burkina Faso, recommended him to Houphouët-Boigny, dictator of Côte d'Ivoire, like he was a choirboy or a saint. Houphouët, who hated Samuel Doe for murdering his son-in-law, was happy to meet Taylor and kissed him right on the mouth. Houphouët and Compaoré quickly agreed that they would support the warlord. Compaoré, on behalf of Burkina Faso, took care of training the soldiers, and Houphouët, on behalf of Côte d'Ivoire, took care of paying for and transporting all the guns.

And that's how Taylor the warlord got to be a big somebody. A famous warlord who bled Liberia dry ('bleed dry' means 'to systematically exploit the population, forcing them to make heavy sacrifices'). Taylor lives in Gbarnea. From time to time, he sends child-soldiers on murderous missions to try and capture the Mansion House. The Mansion House is where the president of Liberia used to live before the warlords divided up the country between them.

Compared to Taylor, Compoaré, the Burkinabé dictator, Houphouët-Boigny, the Ivorian dictator, and Qaddafi, the Libyan dictator, are civilised people, he makes them look like civilised people. Why would they support a barefaced liar, an out-and-out thief, a crook like Taylor and make him head of state? Why? Why? It can only be one of two reasons: either they're as corrupt as Taylor, or they're playing what people in Africa with its barbaric dictatorships and liberticidal fathers of nations call '*la grande politique*'. (According to my *Larousse*, 'liberticidal' means 'that which destroys freedom'.)

In any case, Taylor is always going everywhere pestering everyone. The warlord has taken the whole country hostage and he's so powerful that by the time we arrived in 1993, the slogan his supporters chant, 'No Taylor, No Peace', is becoming a reality. *Gnamokodé! Walahé!*

* * *

Colonel Papa le Bon, Taylor's representative in Zorzor, is weird.

For a start, he never had a father, never knew who his father was. His mother was wandering from bar to bar in the big city of Monrovia when just like that she gave birth to a baby she called Robert's. When the kid was five, a sailor wanted to marry the woman, but he didn't want anything to do with the kid, so Robert's was given to his aunt who also worked in the bars. The aunt used to leave him on his own in the house playing with French letters ('French letters' are condoms).

Some children's rights organisation saw what was happening and took Robert's away and put him in an orphanage run by nuns.

Robert's was a brilliant student. He wanted to be a priest, so they sent him to the USA. When he finished studying he went back to Liberia to be ordained. But it was too late, by now it was tribal war in Liberia. There was nothing left, no Church, no organisations, no records. He wanted to go back to the USA and sit back and wait until things got better.

But when he saw all the street kids everywhere, it reminded him of his childhood and he was deeply moved. So he changed his mind and decided to do something about it. In his soutane, he gathered the kids together and set about making sure they had enough to eat. The kids called him Papa le Bon, which means 'the good father' on account of how he gave food to the street kids.

His work made international repercussions happen and people all over the world wanted to help him and everyone was talking about him but some people weren't happy, especially the dictator Samuel Doe who was still in control in Monrovia. The dictator sent assassins to kill Papa le Bon but he escaped by the skin of his teeth and managed to get to Taylor, who was Doe's sworn enemy. Taylor made Papa le Bon a colonel and gave him lots of power. He put him in charge of a whole district in Zorzor, where he was responsible for collecting the duties and taxes for Taylor.

There were three districts in Zorzor: the top district up in the mountains was where Colonel Papa le Bon ruled everything, the district where the natives' straw huts were, and the refugee district. Refugees had it easier than everyone else in the country because everyone was always giving them food, the UNHCR, NGOs, everyone. But they only allowed women, kids younger than five and old people. In other words I wasn't allowed in. *Gnamokodé!*

The top district was sort of a fortified camp, a compound with human skulls on stakes all round the border and battle stations protected with sandbags. Every station was manned by four child-soldiers. The child-soldiers got lots of good stuff to eat, because if they didn't eat well, they might fuck off and that would be bad for Colonel Papa le Bon. The top district had offices too, and an arsenal, a temple, living quarters and a prison.

The top thing in the top district was the arsenal. The arsenal was sort of a bunker right in the middle of the camp. Colonel Papa le Bon had the keys to the bunker on the belt of his soutane. They were never out of his sight. There were lots of things that were never out of Colonel Papa le Bon's sight: the keys to the arsenal, his kalash and all the grigris he wore to protect him from bullets. *Faforo!* He ate and slept and prayed and did sex stuff wearing the kalash, the keys to the armoury and the grigris that protected him from bullets.

The second most important thing in the top district was the prison. The prison wasn't a real prison. It was a re-education centre. (In the *Petit Robert* it says 're-education' means the act of re-educating, in other words 're-education'. *Walahé!* Even the *Petit Robert* sometimes takes the piss.) In the middle of the prison was the place where Colonel Papa le Bon would cast out the magic from the devourers of souls. It was a centre for exorcism.

There were two separate prisons, one for the men that looked like a real prison with real bars and guards and every-thing. Protecting the men's prison, like everything important that had to be protected, was manned by child-soldiers, virgins. (Virgins are boys who have never done sex. Like me.)

In the prison, everyone was mixed in together: prisoners of war, political prisoners and ordinary prisoners. There was even a category for prisoners that didn't fit into any cate-gory at all: these were the husbands of women that Colonel Papa le Bon had decided to love.

The centre for casting out women was a guesthouse. A luxury guesthouse. Except that the women weren't allowed to come and go whenever they wanted.

The women had to undergo rituals for casting out magic. Colonel Papa le Bon did the casting-out rituals himself, one on one, for hours and hours. Some people said during the rituals, Colonel Papa le Bon took off his clothes and so did the women. *Walahé!*

The third most important thing in the top district was the temple. The temple was for every religion. Every Sunday, everyone in the district had to take part in the papal mass, that's what Colonel Papa le Bon called it. A papal mass because he used the pope's staff. After the mass everyone would listen to Colonel Papa le Bon's sermon.

The sermon was about witchcraft and the evils of witchcraft, about the treachery and the crimes of the other warlords: Johnson, Koroma, Robert Sikié, Samuel Doe, about the martyrdom of the Liberian people at the hands of ULIMO (the United Liberation Movement for Democracy in Liberia), the LPC (the Liberian Peace Council) and NPFL-Koroma.

The temple was also the place where people passing through went to the ecumenical mass. After the ecumenical mass, there was a sermon. It was the same sermon as the one after the papal mass.

Lastly, the fourth most important thing, there were some huts made of straw and corrugated iron, about ten of them. Five of the huts were reserved for Colonel Papa le Bon. No one ever knew where Colonel Papa le Bon spent the night on account of how Colonel Papa le Bon was an important somebody in the tribal wars and nobody ever knows where an important somebody sleeps during tribal wars. That's the rules of tribal wars.

The other five were the barracks where the child-soldiers slept.

Barracks for the child-soldiers, *faforo!* We slept on grass mats right on the floor. And we ate whatever we could, wherever we could.

The village of the natives of Zorzor indigenes was about a kilometre from the entrenched camp. It was made up of huts and houses made of *torchis*, or daub. The people who lived there were Yacous and Gios. Yacou and Gio are the names of the Black Nigger African tribes in this part of the country. The Yacous and the Gios are the sworn enemies of the Guérés and the Krahns. Guéré and Krahn are the names of different Black Nigger African tribes from a different part of fucked-up Liberia. If a Krahn or a Guéré arrived in Zorzor, he had to be tortured and killed because that's the rules of tribal warfare. In tribal warfare, you don't want people around who are from a different tribe from your tribe.

Colonel Papa le Bon had the power of life and death over everyone who lived in Zorzor. He was chief of the town and of the district and above all he was cock of the walk. *Faforo! Walahé!*

As soon as the funeral of the child-soldier Captain Kid was over, we became part of Colonel Papa le Bon's racket.

I was sent to the child-soldier barracks where I got a uniform from an old grown-up Para. It was far too big for me, I was swimming in it. After that, in a solemn ritual, Colonel Papa le Bon himself presented me with a kalash and made me a lieutenant.

They gave child-soldiers ranks so we would be proud. You could be a captain, a commander, a colonel; the lowest rank was lieutenant. My gun was an old AK-47. The colonel taught me how to use it himself. It was dead easy, you just pressed the trigger and it went *tat-tat-tat* and kept killing and killing and all the people would be dropping like flies.

The mother of the dead baby was sent to the guesthouse where the women were exorcised. (To be exorcised, the women had to be locked up naked one on one with Colonel Papa le Bon. That was the rules of tribal wars.)

Colonel Papa le Bon was really happy to have Yacouba, very happy to have a grigriman, a top-notch Muslim grigriman.

'What sort of grigris do you make?' Colonel Papa le Bon asked him.

'All sorts,' Yacouba told him.

'Can you make grigris that protect against bullets?'

'I'm really good at bullet-proofing. That's why I came to Liberia where there's tribal wars and bullets flying all over the place killing people without warning.'

'Excellent! Excellent!' roared Colonel Papa le Bon.

He kissed Yacouba on the mouth and put him in one of the huts reserved for important somebodies. Yacouba was blessed. He had everything and most of all he ate enough for four people.

Yacouba got to work straight away and made three grigris – one, two, three – for Colonel Papa le Bon. Top-notch grigris. The first one was for the morning, the second for the afternoon and the third for the night-time. Colonel Papa le Bon attached them to the belt of his soutane. And paid cash. Yacouba whispered in his ear – for his ears only – the interdictions attached to each grigri (an 'interdiction' is a law that forbids you from doing something). Yacouba set himself up as a shaman. He made prophecies, tracing lines in the sand that revealed Colonel Papa le Bon's future. He told the colonel he had to sacrifice two oxen. Two big bulls.

'But there are no bulls in Zorzor,' answered Colonel Papa le Bon.

'You must do this; it is a necessary sacrifice. It is written in your future. But it's not really, really urgent,' said Yacouba.

Yacouba made grigris for all the child-soldiers and all the grown-up soldiers. He sold the grigris for lots of money. I got the most powerful grigris and Yacouba gave me mine free! All the grigris had to be renewed, so Yacouba was never short of work. Never! Yacouba was as rich as Moro-naba. Moro-naba was the name of the rich chief of the Mossis of Burkina-Faso. Yacouba sent money back to his village, to Togobala, to his parents, to the *griots* and the *almami* (a '*griot*' is a traditional historian, a praise singer, and an '*almami*' is a religious leader, according to the *Glossary*) on account of how he had so much money to spare.

Daytime only lasts about twelve hours. It was a shame, a terrible shame, twelve hours just weren't enough for Colonel Papa le Bon. There was always work left over for tomorrow. Allah should have been merciful and made fifty-hour days for Colonel Papa le Bon. Fifty whole hours. *Walahé!*

Every morning Colonel Papa le Bon woke up at cockcrow — except on the mornings after he'd drunk too much good palm wine before going to bed. But I can tell you that he never smoked hash. Never, ever. Every morning he changed his grigris, put on his white soutane and his kalash. Then he took the papal staff with the crucifix on top, a crucifix decorated with a rosary and started by inspecting the battle stations. The watchtowers inside the camp manned by child-soldiers and the watchtowers outside manned by real soldiers.

Every morning he went into the temple and officiated. ('Officiate' is a big word that means 'to conduct a religious ceremony', that's what it says in my *Larousse*.) He officiated with altar boys who were child-soldiers. Afterwards he had breakfast, but no alcohol. Alcohol wasn't good for Colonel Papa le Bon early in the morning. It fucked up his whole day.

Afterwards, still wearing his soutane, Colonel Papa le Bon would hand out the day's ration of grain to the soldiers' wives. He had a set of mechanical scales. He'd talk to each soldier's wife, and sometimes he'd burst out laughing and if she was really pretty he'd give her a slap on the arse. That was Colonel Papa le Bon's fixed schedule, the schedule of things he had to do no matter what, even if he was laid up with malaria, even if he'd been drinking good palm wine. Only after he had distributed the grain to the soldiers' wives and the child-soldiers' cooks could he do other stuff depending on what day it was.

If he had to give a ruling or if there was a trial, he would stay in the temple until noon. The temple was also the courthouse on account of how the accused had to swear by God and by the grigris. It was trial by ordeal, which means 'a barbarous, medieval method of justice'. Justice took place once a week, usually on Saturdays.

If Colonel Papa le Bon had no ruling to make, then right

after he had distributed the grain, he went straight to the infirmary. After their medicine, the doctor brought all the sick and the lame and the other fucked-up patients into one room where Colonel Papa le Bon preached to them, and he preached hard. It wasn't unusual to see a sick person throw away his crutches and shout 'I'm cured!' and start walking around just like a normal person. *Walahé!* Colonel Papa le Bon was a seriously good and expert preacher.

After the infirmary Colonel Papa le Bon supervised the military training of the child-soldiers and the real soldiers. Military training was a bit like religious training or civic training and all of them were pretty much the same as the sermon. If you truly loved the Lord God and Jesus Christ, bullets wouldn't hit you; they'd kill other people instead, because it is God alone who kills the bad guys, the arseholes, the sinners and the damned.

All this work for just one man – Colonel Papa le Bon did all this work by himself. *Walahé!* It was too much.

And then there were the convoys we ambushed from time to time. Sometimes Colonel Papa le Bon personally weighed the luggage and haggled with the passengers and collected the duties and taxes and put them in the pockets of his soutane.

And then there were the exorcisms. And the meetings . . . and the . . . and the mountain of paperwork that Colonel Papa le Bon had to sign as supreme commander of the NPFL for the eastern section of the Republic of Liberia.

And then there were all sorts of spies.

Colonel Papa le Bon deserved to have a fifty-hour day! *Faforo!* A full fifty-hour day.

Of course, Colonel Papa le Bon deserved to spend some of the countless stinking nights in this dog's life in Zorzor getting drunk. But he never smoked hash. The hash was reserved for the child-soldiers, on account of it made them as strong as real soldiers. *Walahé!*

When I first got to the camp, they explained to me who I was. I was a Mandingo, a Muslim, friend of the Yacous and the Gios. In Black American pidgin, Malinké and Mandingo are *kif-kif*, same difference. I was happy that I wasn't a Guéré or a Krahn. Colonel Papa le Bon didn't like the Guérés and the Krahns. He put them to death.

Because of Yacouba the grigriman, everyone spoiled me and looked out for me. I was singled out by Colonel Papa le Bon who appointed me captain, to replace poor Kid on account of how I was the grigriman's boy, his kid, so everyone thought I had the best protection.

The colonel appointed me captain and my duties were to stand in the middle of the road and signal for the trucks and convoys to stop. I was the ambush kid, so I got lots to eat and sometimes I got given hash for free, gratis. The first time I smoked hash, I puked like a sick dog, but after a while I got used to it and soon it made me strong as a grown-up. *Faforo!*

I had a friend, a child-soldier called Commander Jean Taï, or Tête Brûlée on account of him being a hot-head. Tête Brûlée had escaped from ULIMO and stole lots of AK-47s. Because he showed up at the camp with lots of guns, Colonel Papa le Bon made him a commander. Back at ULIMO he pretended to be a Krahn but actually he was pure-blood Yacou. He got a big welcome to the NPFL from Colonel Papa le Bon because he turned up with kalashes he stole from ULIMO and because he wasn't a Krahn.

Commander Tête Brûlée was a good guy. The best. *Walahé!* He lied more than he breathed. He was a fabulist. (According to my *Larousse*, a 'fabulist' is someone who makes up stories that are total lies.) Commander Tête Brûlée was a fabulist. He'd done everything and everything. And seen everything. He'd even met my aunt and talked to her. This made me feel relieved. I had to get to ULIMO as soon as possible.

The little liar told a lot of stories about ULIMO. He said lots of good things about ULIMO and the stories made everyone want to go to ULIMO where everything was cool and everyone had it easy. You could eat like a horse and there was always leftovers. You could sleep all day and every month they gave you a salary. He knew what he was talking about: a salary! At the end of every month they just gave you the salary, sometimes even before the end of the month, on account of how ULIMO had lots of American dollars because they exploited a lot of mines. Some of the mines were gold and some were diamonds and there were other mines of precious metals. The soldiers guarded the miners, the miners worked in the mines, and the soldiers got to eat lots of food and even got American dollars to keep for themselves. The child-soldiers had it even better. They had beds and brand new Para uniforms and new kalashes. *Walahé!*

Commander Tête Brûlée was sorry he'd left ULIMO. He came to our camp because he was one hundred percent

Yacou, and back there he had to pretend he was a Krahn. He came to our camp because someone told him his mother and father were hiding in Zorzor, but he didn't find them because it wasn't true. Now he was just waiting for a chance to go back to ULIMO. Everything was cool at ULIMO, everyone had it easy.

Colonel Papa le Bon got wind of the things Tête Brûlée was saying. (To 'get wind of' means 'to hear about something from someone else', according to my *Petit Robert*.) Colonel Papa le Bon got wind of Commander Tête Brûlée's barefaced lies. He was really angry and he sent for Tête Brûlée and bawled him out like a rotten fish. He threatened him and said that if he kept on saying good things about ULIMO and saying ULIMO was like heaven on earth then he'd throw him in jail.

It didn't work. Tête Brûlée just kept on brainwashing us all behind Colonel Papa le Bon's back. ('Brainwashing' is a big word. According to my *Larousse*, it means 'forcible indoctrination into a new set of attitudes and beliefs'.)

Colonel Papa le Bon, in his goodness, built an orphanage for girls. It was for girls who had lost their parents in the tribal wars and it was only for girls younger than seven. Little girls who had nothing to eat and not enough breasts to get a husband or be a child-soldier. It was a great charitable work for girls younger than seven. The orphanage was run by nuns who taught the girls writing, reading and religion.

The nuns wore cornets to fool the outside world (a 'cornet' is a starched white headdress, often cone-shaped, worn by nuns), but actually, like all the other women, they made love – they did it with Colonel Papa le Bon. Because Colonel Papa le Bon was the number-one rooster in the henhouse and because that's the way things are in real life.

So, one morning, one of the girls was found raped and murdered on the edge of the track that led to the river. A little seven-year-old girl raped and murdered. It was such an agonising thing that Colonel Papa le Bon cried his heart out. You should have seen it – Colonel Papa le Bon, a complete *ouya-ouya*, crying his heart out (according to the *Glossary*, '*ouya-ouya*' means 'a bum, a good-for-nothing'). It was worth seeing.

There was a funeral vigil and Colonel Papa le Bon offici-ated himself with his soutane, his colonel's stripes, his grigris under his clothes, his kalash and the papal staff. Colonel Papa le Bon danced a lot and drank a little. On account of alcohol isn't very good for Colonel Papa le Bon. After the dancing, he turned around three times, studied the sky four times, then walked forward to the soldier directly in front of him. He took the soldier's hand, the soldier stood up and Colonel Papa le Bon led him into the centre of the circle. The soldier's name was Zemoko. Zemoko was not innocent: either he was guilty of the death of the little girl or he knew who was responsible for her death. Colonel Papa le Bon repeated the ritual, walked forward and pointed to another soldier. The soldier's name was Wourouda. Wourouda was guilty of the death of the little girl or he knew who was responsible for her death. Colonel Papa le Bon did the trick a third time, walked forward and led Commander Tête Brûlée into the middle of the circle. Tête Brûlée was guilty of the death of the little girl or he knew who was responsible for her death. Tête Brûlée and the two soldiers were mixed up in the girl's death. They were immediately arrested, even though they protested their innocence. ('To protest one's innocence' means to 'avow formally or solemnly that one is innocent', according to my *Larousse*.)

The next day, the court was in session to judge the murderers of the little girl.

Colonel Papa le Bon was there wearing his soutane and all his medals, with his Bible and his Qur'an on hand. The spectators sat in the nave like they do for a mass. An ecumenical mass. Even though this wasn't a mass, the judgement started with a prayer. Then, Colonel Papa le Bon asked the defendants to swear on the holy books three times. The defendants swore.

'Zemoko, did you kill Fati?' asked Colonel Papa le Bon.

'I swear on the Bible that it wasn't me, it wasn't me.'

'Wourouda, did you kill Fati?'

Wourouda said it wasn't him.

Colonel Papa le Bon put the same question to Tête Brûlée and got the same answer.

Next came the ordeal. A knife was put into a fire of glowing coals until the blade was white-hot, then each defendant opened his mouth and stuck out his tongue. Colonel Papa le Bon took the white-hot blade and ran it over Zemoko's tongue. Zemoko didn't flinch; he closed his mouth and went back to his seat in the nave. The audience clapped. Then it was Wourouda's turn. The audience clapped when Wourouda closed his mouth without flinching. But when Colonel Papa le Bon's blade came towards Tête Brûlée, Commander Tête Brûlée jumped back and ran out of the church. A roar of surprise erupted from the crowd. Commander Tête Brûlée was quickly caught and overpowered.

He was guilty; he had killed poor Fati. Tête Brûlée made a clean breast and admitted everything, he said the devil had entered him and guided his actions.

He was sentenced to submit himself to the rituals of exorcism for two whole rainy seasons. If the devil within him was too powerful, if the rituals did not succeed in casting out the devil in his body, he would be executed. Publicly executed. With an AK-47. If the exorcism worked, he would be pardoned by Colonel Papa le Bon, because Colonel Papa le Bon, with his papal staff, is righteousness itself. But . . . But he could not be a child-soldier any more, because a child-soldier who has raped and murdered isn't a virgin and when you're not a virgin you can't be one of Colonel Papa le Bon's child-soldiers. That's the way it is; there's no arguing. You have to be a soldier. A proper soldier, a grown-up soldier.

Grown-up soldiers are not given any food or anywhere to sleep and they don't get any salary at all. Being a child-soldier had its advantages. *Walahé!* We were privileged. If Tête Brûlée escaped being executed, he couldn't be a child-soldier any more because he wasn't a virgin. *Gnamokodé!*

Faforo! Right now we were miles from Zorzor, miles and miles from Colonel Papa le Bon's camp. The sun had hopped up like a cricket and *doni-doni* it was starting to rise (according to the *Glossary*, '*doni-doni*' means 'little by little'). We had to be careful and take small steps. We were only a few metres from the forest. We had to elude the NPFL soldiers ('elude' means 'to cunningly avoid'). The soldiers might follow us. We made the most of the moonlight to go far, to go fast, to make ourselves scarce.

We had left the camp the night before, foot to the road, out of Zorzor. At about eleven o'clock, Colonel Papa le Bon had been assassinated, gunned down, he was dead. Even with all his grigris, he gave up the ghost. To tell the truth, when I saw Colonel Papa le Bon dead it made me feel sick because I thought he was immortal, because Colonel Papa le Bon had been good to me. To everyone. And he was a phenomenon of nature ('phenomenon' means 'an unusual or unaccountable fact or event, a remarkable or outstanding person').

Colonel Papa le Bon's death was the signal, the *shofar* of freedom for the prisoners. (A '*shofar*' is a trumpet made of a ram's horn.) The prisoners who were there to be cast out, the prisoners who were there for love. It was the signal for everyone who wanted to escape to leave, even the soldiers and the child-soldiers. Lots of the child-soldiers hadn't found their parents at NPFL and thought they might find them at ULIMO. And anyway, over at ULIMO they had lots of food. Over at ULIMO you got to eat *riz gras* with *sauce graine*. At ULIMO everyone got a salary and it arrived smack bang on time, like mangoes in April. *Faforo!*

It wasn't easy to escape from the camp. We had to fight the *ouya-ouyas* who were still loyal to the NPFL. All the arse-holes who still thought things were better with Colonel Papa le Bon. But in the end, we won. So then we pillaged everything, smashed everything, torched everything. And right after that we set off. Like a flash, at the double.

We were all carrying the spoils of our pillaging. Some people had two or even three kalashes. The AK-47s would make good corroboration for ULIMO ('corroboration' means 'proof'). It would prove to ULIMO that we left the NPFL on bad, really bad, terms and prove how much we really wanted to join ULIMO. We looted everything and then we torched the place.

As soon as Colonel Papa le Bon had been gunned down, soldiers cried out in the night, 'Colonel Papa le Bon is dead . . . Papa le Bon is dead. The colonel has been murdered . . . murdered!' It made a hell of a ruckus (a disturbance or a commotion). It was the soldiers that started the looting. They looted all the money; they looted the soutanes; they looted the grain; they mainly looted the store of hash . . . They had looted all and everything before the loyal soldiers started shooting.

Walahé! Let's start at the start.

One day when he was searching the luggage from a convoy, Colonel Papa le Bon found lots of bottles of whisky, Johnny Walker Red Label, good shit. And, instead of making the guy pay lots of duties and taxes, Colonel Papa le Bon took three bottles for himself. Alcohol wasn't good for Colonel Papa le Bon. He knew that, so he only allowed himself alcohol on hardly any nights and only when he was really, really tired and his head was all muddled. He drank when he went to bed and the next morning he would wake up a bit late, a bit sick. But it wasn't too bad, because the colonel never smoked hash: he kept all the hash for the child-soldiers because it was good for them and made them as strong as real soldiers. That night (the night he got the bottles of whisky), Colonel Papa le Bon was sincerely tired and he didn't even wait until he went to bed to drink his whisky, too much whisky. Alcohol made Colonel Papa le Bon fucked up in the head.

Inebriated with alcohol, Colonel Papa le Bon headed off to the prison ('inebriated' means 'under the influence'). Inebriated, Colonel Papa le Bon headed off on his own – all on his own – to the prison, somewhere he never went even in the daytime unless he had two child-soldiers armed to the teeth to protect him.

In the prison, alone in the night, he laughed with the prisoners, chatted with the prisoners, and joked with Tête Brûlée.

At some point, things turned sour ('turn sour' means 'take a turn for the worse'). Colonel Papa le Bon started roaring like a wild beast the way he sometimes did. Colonel Papa le Bon staggered around like a madman and shouted 'I'm going to kill the lot of you. I'm going to kill the lot of you . . .' and then he cackled like a hyena in the darkness. 'That's how it goes . . . that's how it goes . . . I'm going to kill you all.' He unbuckled his kalash from under his soutane and fired into the air twice. At first the prisoners ran away and hid in the corners. Still standing, still staggering, he fired two more times and then he went quiet for a minute, he was sleepy. In the half-light, one of the prisoners cautiously crawled up behind Colonel Papa le Bon and threw himself at the colonel's feet knocking him down. The kalash slipped out of his hands and skidded far, far away in front of him. Tête Brûlée grabbed the gun and fired at Colonel Papa le Bon who was lying right on the ground. He emptied the magazine into him on account of Tête Brûlée is fucked up in the head.

Faforo! The bullets went straight through Colonel Papa le Bon, even though he was wearing Yacouba's grigris. Yacouba explained that it was because Colonel Papa le Bon had violated the proscriptions attached to the grigris. Number one, you're not allowed to wear the grigris when you are making love. Number two, after making love, you have to wash before you tie on the grigris. But Colonel Papa le Bon made love all the time, every way possible, and didn't have time to wash himself. And there was another reason. The colonel had never sacrificed the two bulls written in his destiny. If he had sacrificed the two bulls, he would never have wandered into the prison on his own. The sacrifice of the bulls would have prevented the circumstance from happening. *Faforo!*

As soon as Colonel Papa le Bon is dead, good and dead, one of the prisoners turns over his body and grabs the keys to the arsenal. Colonel Papa le Bon always kept the keys to the arsenal on him at all times. For the prisoners and the soldiers who wanted to go to ULIMO, this was the *shofar* of freedom, but there were some people who didn't want to leave, people who were still loyal to the NPFL and to Colonel Papa le Bon. There was a battle between the two groups and in the end the ones who wanted to leave managed to fuck off.

Yacouba and me, we wanted to go to ULIMO because ULIMO was in Niangbo and Niangbo was where my aunt lived. My aunt had managed to contact Yacouba and tell him that she was there, and Commander Tête Brûlée had even seen my aunt there even if it's true that Tête Brûlée was a pathological liar and you should never believe a word a pathological liar says.

We followed Tête Brûlée because he was the one who knew how to find the nearest ULIMO post. There were thirty-seven of us, sixteen child-soldiers, twenty grown-up soldiers and Yacouba. We were all loaded up with guns and ammunition and not too much food. Tête Brûlée had us all believing that ULIMO was really close, right round the next bend. But it wasn't true, the kid was a liar. It took at least two or three days to get to the nearest ULIMO post. And the others were hot on our heels. (To be hot on someone's heels means to be following them.) Luckily, there were lots of different routes to ULIMO and they didn't know which route we took. All of us were from different tribes, but we knew that to get into ULIMO you had to be a Krahn or a Guéré. Only Krahns and Guérés were allowed into ULIMO. So everyone took a Krahn name. I didn't have to change my name, I was Malinké, what like the Black Americans in Liberia call Mandingo. The Malinkés or Mandingos are always welcome wherever we go because we're out-and-out defectors. We're always changing sides.

It was a long road and we had too much ammunition and too many guns. We couldn't carry everything, so we dumped some kalashes and some of the ammunition.

With all the hash, we got hungrier and hungrier. Hash isn't good when you're hungry. So we ate all the fruit we could find and after that we ate roots and after that leaves. And even after all that Yacouba still said Allah in his infinite goodness never leaves empty a mouth he has created.

One of the child-soldiers was a girl soldier, her name was Sarah. Sarah was unique, she was pretty as four girls put together and she smoked enough hash for ten. For a long time back in Zorzor, she had been Tête Brûlée's secret girlfriend. That's why she came with us. Ever since we left Zorzor, they (she and Tête Brûlée) hadn't stopped stopping to kiss each other. And every time we stopped she'd smoke some more hash and munch some more grass. We had hash and grass in abundance. In abundance because we'd cleaned out Colonel Papa le Bon's stockpile. And she smoked and munched incessantly ('incessantly' means 'without stopping', according to my *Larousse*). She went completely crazy and started touching her *gnoussou-gnoussou* in front of everyone and asking Tête Brûlée to make love to her in public in front of everyone. But Tête Brûlée said no because we were in a hurry and we were hungry. Sarah wanted to rest. She slumped against a tree trunk to rest. Tête Brûlée really loved Sarah and he didn't want to just leave her like that but we had people following us and we couldn't hang about. Tête Brûlée tried to make her to stand up and come with us and she fired a whole clip cartridge at Tête Brûlée. Luckily she was all drugged up and she couldn't see for shit so the bullets just disappeared into the air. In a rage, Tête Brûlée retaliated. He fired at her legs and disarmed her. She screamed like a suckling calf, like a stuck pig. And Tête Brûlée got all miserable, completely miserable.

We had to leave her there all alone, we had to abandon her to her sad fate, but Tête Brûlée couldn't bring himself to do it. Sarah screamed her maman's name and God's name and everything and Tête Brûlée went over to her and kissed her and he started crying. We left them there kissing, with arms round each other and crying and off we went, foot to the road. We hadn't got very far when Tête Brûlée showed up on his own, still crying. He had left Sarah alone beside the tree, alone with all her blood and all her wounds. The bitch ('bitch' means a cruel, wicked girl) couldn't walk any more. The army ants and the vultures would make a real feast of her.

According to my *Larousse*, a funeral oration is a speech in honour of a famous celebrity who's dead. Child-soldiers are the most famous celebrities of the late twentieth century, so whenever a child-soldier dies, we have to say a funeral oration. That means we have to recount how in this great big fucked-up world they came to be a child-soldier. I do it when I feel like it, but I don't have to. I'm doing it for Sarah because I want to, I've got the time, and anyway it's interesting.

Sarah's father was called Bouaké; he was a sailor. He travelled and travelled, he did nothing but travel so much that you wonder how he found time to make Sarah in her mother's belly. Her mother sold rotten fish in the big market in Monrovia and sometimes she looked after her daughter. When Sarah was five, her mother was knocked down by a drunk driver and killed. Her father didn't know what you're supposed to do with girls, so he gave her to his cousin in a remote village, who gave her to Madame Kokui. Madame Kokui had a shop and she had five children. She put Sarah to work cleaning and selling bananas in the street. Every morning, after she finished washing the dishes and washing the clothes, she walked the streets of Monrovia selling bananas and came home at six on the dot to put the stockpot on the fire and bath the baby. Madame Kokui was very pernickety about the accounts and very strict about what time Sarah got home. ('Pernickety' and 'strict' both mean 'hard to please'.)

One morning, a little boy, a street kid, stole a bunch of bananas and made a run for it. Sarah ran after the little boy, but she didn't catch him. When she got back to the house, she explained what had happened, but Madame Kokui wasn't happy, not one bit. She screamed at Sarah and accused her of selling the bananas and buying sweets with all the money. Sarah told her it was the little boy who took them, but it was no use. Madame Kokui was still angry and wouldn't listen to her. She whipped Sarah and locked her in her room with no supper and she said, 'Next time, I'll whip you a lot harder and I'll lock you up for a whole day with no food.'

Next time was the next day. Like every morning, Sarah went out with her load of bananas. The same little boy showed up with a gang of friends, snatched a bunch of bananas and ran off. Sarah ran after him. That's what his friends were waiting for on account of they were just as much brats as him. When Sarah ran after him, they swiped the rest of the bananas ('swipe' means 'to steal, to make off with', according to my *Larousse*).

Sarah was in tears. She cried all day long, but when the sun started setting and she knew it would soon be time to go home and bath the baby, she decided to beg. To beg to get the money to pay back Madame Kokui. But sadly the drivers she begged from weren't very generous and she didn't have enough to pay back Madame Kokui, so that night she slept in the doorway of a shop called Farah among all the packages.

The next day she went begging again, but it wasn't until the day after that that she finally got enough money to pay back Madame Kokui and by then it was too late. She couldn't go back to the house now on account of how she'd already spent two nights sleeping rough. If she went back, Madame Kokui would kill her, kill her stone dead. So Sarah kept on begging and after a while she got used to the circumstances, and figured out she was better off begging than she had been with Madame Kokui. She found somewhere to wash, and another place where she could hide her savings and she went on sleeping in the doorway of Farah among the packages and the boxes.

She had been spotted there by a man, and one day he came and found her in the doorway of Farah. He introduced himself, he was kind and sympathetic. ('Sympathetic' means he pretended like he cared about Sarah's problems.) He offered Sarah sweets and other stuff so Sarah trusted him and followed him to a covered market far away from the houses. That's where he told her that he was going to make love to her gently and not hurt her. Sarah was scared and she started running and screaming, but the man was a lot faster and a lot stronger and he caught up with Sarah and knocked her down and forced her on to the ground and raped her. He was so vicious that he left Sarah for dead.

Sarah was taken to hospital and when she woke up the nurse asked her who her parents were. She told the nurse about her father, but not about Madame Kokui. The hospital people tried to find her father but they didn't find him. He was travelling; he was always travelling. They sent Sarah to the nuns at the orphanage in the suburbs west of Monrovia and that's where she was living when the tribal wars got started. Five of the nuns in the orphanage were massacred; the others got the fuck out on the double, no questions asked. Sarah and four of her friends had been prostitutes before they joined the child-soldiers, so as not to starve to death.

That's Sarah, who we left to the army ants and the vultures. (According to the *Glossary*, army ants are black ants that are really, really voracious.) They were going to make a delicious feast of her. *Gnamokodé!*

All the villages along the way were deserted, one hundred percent deserted. That's the way it goes in tribal wars: everyone abandons the villages where humans live and go and live in the forests where the wild beasts live. Wild beasts have a better life than people. *Faforo!*

As we came in to one of the deserted villages, we spotted two guys who took off, made a run for it like they were robbers. We chased after them, because that's what you're supposed to do in tribal wars. When you see someone and they run away, that means they're trying to hurt you so you have to catch them first. The two guys had vanished into the forest. We fired lots and lots of bullets. It made an awful ruckus; it sounded like the Samorian wars all over again. (Samory was a Malinké chief who resisted the French invasions and whose *sofas* – soldiers – did lots of shooting.) *Walahé!*

One of the child-soldiers was a captain who was unique and everyone called him 'Captain Kik the Cunning'. Captain Kik the Cunning was weird. While we were just standing there by the roadside, Kik the Cunning ran right into the forest and headed left to try and cut off the fugitives' path back to the village. It was cunning. But then, suddenly, we heard an explosion, and then Kik was screaming. We all rushed to him. Kik had stepped on a mine. It was a terrible sight. Kik was screaming like a suckling calf, like a stuck pig. He was screaming for his mum, for his dad, for all and everyone. His leg was in bloody shreds and hanging by a thread. It was a sorry sight. He was sweating huge drops of sweat and bawling, 'I'm gonna die! I'm gonna die like a fly!' A kid like that, giving up the ghost like that, it's not a pretty sight. We made a makeshift stretcher.

Kik was carried back to the village on the makeshift stretcher. One of the soldiers had once been a nurse. The nurse thought Kik should be amputated immediately, at once. Back in the village, we laid Kik on the floor of one of the huts. It took three guys to hold him down. He screamed, he struggled, he called for his maman, but the nurse cut off his leg anyway, right at the knee. Right at the knee. He threw the leg to a passing dog. We propped Kik up against the wall of the hut.

Then we started searching all the huts. One by one. Thoroughly. The villagers had run away as soon as they heard the machine-gun bullets we were firing. We were hungry and we needed something to eat. We found chickens. We chased them and caught them and wrung their necks and then we roasted them. There were kid goats wandering around too. We slaughtered them and roasted them too. We took anything worth eating. Allah never leaves empty a mouth he has created.

We searched every nook and cranny. We thought there was nobody there, absolutely nobody, so we were surprised to find two cute kids whose mother hadn't been able to take them with her in her frantic escape ('frantic' means 'violent and desperate', according to my *Larousse*). She just abandoned them, and the two kids had hidden under some branches in a pen.

Among the child-soldiers there was a girl named Fati. Like all the girl soldiers, Fati was really cruel. Like all the girl soldiers, Fati smoked too much hash and was always fucked up. Fati dragged the two kids out of their hidey-hole under the branches and ordered them to show us where the villagers hid their food. The kids didn't understand a word, not one word. They were too little. It was twins and they were only about six years old. They were scared. They didn't understand what was going on. Fati decided to scare them, decided to fire her machine-gun into the air but, on account of she was totally fucked up on hash, she completely machine-gunned the kids with her AK-47, leaving one of them dead and the other one wounded. The bullets had ripped his whole arm off. Fati broke down and cried because you're not supposed to hurt twins, especially little twins. The *gnamas* of twins, especially when they're still kids, are terrifying. (*'Gnamas'* are the shadows, the avenging spirits of the dead.) *Gnamas* like that never forgive. It was sad, really sad. Fati would be forever hunted by *gnamas*, the *gnamas* of little twins, and all because of the fucked-up tribal wars in Liberia. She was finished; she was going to die a terrible death.

Yacouba told Fati that the grigris would not protect her any more on account of the little twins' *gnamas.*

Fati cried, she cried her heart out, she howled like a spoiled brat; she wanted proper grigris. But even though she cried, Fati was done for; she had no grigris to protect her. That's how it goes.

After accidentally going and murdering two innocent kids, we couldn't stay in the village, we had to get out of there fast, get out *gnona-gnona* (according to the *Glossary*, '*gnona-gnona*' means 'on the double'). We left Kik leaning against the wall of a hut and ran off, foot to the road, *gnona-gnona*.

We left Kik to the mercy of humans in the village the way we left Sarah to the mercy of the animals and the insects. Which of them was better off? Definitely not Kik. That's wars for you. Animals have more mercy for the wounded than humans.

OK, since we knew that Kik was going to die, that he was as good as dead, we had to do his funeral oration. I'd like to tell it because Kik was a nice kid and his passage wasn't long. ('Passage' is the path a kid follows in his whole short life on earth, according to my *Larousse*.)

89

The tribal wars arrived in Kik's village at about ten o'clock in the morning. The children were at school and their parents were at home. Kik was at school and his parents were at home. When they heard the first bursts of gunfire, the children ran into the forest. Kik ran into the forest. And the kids stayed in the forest all the time they could hear the gunfire from the village. Kik stayed in the forest. It was only the next morning when there was no more noise that the children dared to go back to their family huts. Kik went back to his family hut and found his father's throat cut, his brother's throat cut, his mother and his sister raped and their heads bashed in. All of his relatives, close and distant, dead. And when you've got no one left on earth, no father, no mother, no brother, no sister, and you're really young, just a little kid, living in some fucked-up barbaric country where everyone is cutting everyone's throat, what do you do?

You become a child-soldier of course, a small-soldier, a child-soldier so you can have lots to eat and cut some throats yourself; that's all your only option.

Gradually, Kik became a child-soldier. (According to my *Larousse*, 'gradually' means 'continuing steadily by increments', one thing or one word or one action leading to another.) Kik was cunning. The cunning child-soldier took a shortcut. Taking a shortcut, he stepped on a mine. We had carried him on a makeshift stretcher and propped him up, dying, against the wall of a hut. We had abandoned him, left him, dying, in the middle of the afternoon in some fucked-up village, to the tender mercies of the villagers. ('Tender mercies' doesn't mean what it says; it means 'attention or treatment not in the best interests of its recipients'.) To their tender mercies, because that's how Allah decided he wanted poor Kik to end his days on earth. Allah is not obliged to be fair about everything, about all his creations, about all his actions here on earth.

The same goes for me. I don't have to talk, I'm not obliged to tell my dog's-life-story, wading through dictionary after dictionary. I'm fed up talking, so I'm going to stop for today. You can all fuck off!

Walahé! Faforo! Gnamokodé!

3

ULIMO is the name of the faction loyal to the bandit warlord President-Dictator Samuel Doe, who got himself hacked limb from limb. He was torn limb from limb on a misty afternoon in Monrovia the terrible, capital of the Republic of Liberia, independent since 1860. *Walahé!*

The dictator Samuel Doe started off as a sergeant in the Liberian army. He – Sergeant Doe – and some of his friends were fed up with the arrogance and the contempt that the Black Nigger Afro-Americans, or Congos, showed for the indigenous people of Liberia. 'Indigenous people' are the Black Nigger African Natives 'originating and living or occurring naturally in an area'. They're different from Black Nigger Afro-Americans who are 'descendants of freed slaves'. The descendants of the slaves, also known as Congos, acted just like the colonists in Liberia. That's how my *Harrap's* defines 'indigenous people' and 'Afro-Americans'. Samuel Doe and some of his friends were fed up of all the injustice that rained down on the indigenous people of Liberia in independent Liberia. That was why the indigenous people revolted and it was why two indigenous people plotted an indigenous conspiracy against the arrogant colonials and the Afro-American colonialists.

The two indigenous people, the two Black Nigger African indigenes who organised the military coup were Samuel Doe, a Krahn, and Thomas Quionkpa, a Gio. The Krahns and the Gios are the two main Black Nigger African tribes in Liberia. That's why people say the whole of independent Liberia rose up against the arrogant colonials and the Afro-American colonialists.

Luckily for them (the rebels), or maybe because they made fitting sacrifices, the military coup was a complete success. (According to the *Glossary*, 'fitting sacrifices' means that Black Nigger African Natives make lots of bloodthirsty sacrifices for good luck, but they only have good luck if their sacrifices are fitting.) After the success of the military coup, the two rebels and their followers dragged all the VIPs, all the Afro-American senators from their beds and took them all down to the beach. On the beach, they stripped them down to their underpants and tied them to stakes. When the sun came up, they shot them like rabbits, in front of the international press. Then the conspirators went back to the city. In the city, they massacred the wives and children of the men they'd shot and had a huge carnival with lots of hullabaloo, outrageousness, drunkenness, etc.

Afterwards, the two chief conspirators kissed each other on the lips like civilised men and clapped each other on the back. Sergeant Samuel Doe promoted Thomas Quionkpa to the rank of general, and Sergeant Thomas Quionkpa promoted Sergeant Samuel Doe to the rank of general. But since there could only be one leader, one head of state, Samuel Doe declared himself president and undisputed and undisputable leader of the unitary and democratic Republic of Liberia founded in 1860.

It came at exactly the right moment, just like salt in soup, because it happened just before a summit of heads of state of the CDEAO (Community of West African States). Liberia is part of the CDEAO. Samuel Doe, with his general's rank and his title of head of state and his Para uniform and his pistol hanging from his belt, jumped on a plane. He jumped straight on to a plane as head of state to take part in the summit of heads of state of the CDEAO. The summit took place in Lomé. But in Lomé, things turned sour. When Doe arrived armed to the teeth, the CDEAO heads of state got scared. They thought he was a lunatic so wouldn't allow him into the summit. No way. They locked him up in a hotel for the duration of the summit with a complete ban on sticking his nose out the door or drinking any alcohol. After the summit was over they stuck him back on his plane and sent him off to Monrovia, his capital. Like an *ouya-ouya*.

Samuel Doe ruled peacefully from his capital, Monrovia, for five whole rainy seasons. He went round in his Para uniform with his pistol on his belt like a hundred percent rebel. But one day he thought about Thomas Quionkpa and he frowned, suddenly he felt uncomfortable in his Para uniform. Don't forget Samuel Doe did his military coup with Thomas Quionkpa and Thomas Quionkpa was still alive. Even a chicken-thief will tell you: if you pull off a big robbery with someone, you will never truly enjoy the spoils until the other person is dead. After five years in power, the fact that Thomas Quionkpa was still alive was still an evil influence on the morale, the words and the actions of General Samuel Doe.

To sort things out, Samuel Doe came up with a foolproof stratagem. ('Stratagem' means 'a trick designed to deceive an enemy', according to my *Petit Robert*.) It was simple when you thought about it. Doe used the democratic stratagem. Democracy, the voice of the people, the sovereign will of the people. All that shit . . .

One Saturday morning, Samuel Doe decreed a carnival and summoned all the field officers in the Liberian army, and all the ministers in his administration and the heads of all the cantons in the republic and all the religious leaders. In front of this areopagus (an 'areopagus' is a meeting with lots of clever people), he made a speech.

'I took power by force of arms, because in this country there was too much injustice. Now that everyone in the country is equal and justice has been restored, the military should no longer rule. The military will hand over to a civilian government, to the sovereign people. I hereby solemnly renounce my military rank, my military uniform, my pistol. I hereby become a civilian.'

He took off his pistol, his Para's uniform, his red beret,

his shirt with all his medals, his trousers, his shoes and his socks. He stripped down to his underpants. Then he clicked his fingers and an orderly appeared. The orderly brought him a three-piece suit, a shirt, a tie, socks, shoes and a trilby hat. And, to the applause of everyone present, he dressed as a civilian, just like an ordinary *ouya-ouya* on a street corner.

After that, things moved fast. In three weeks, Samuel Doe had a constitution made to measure. He spent two months travelling to every district in Liberia explaining how good everything was. Then one Sunday morning, the constitution was adopted with 99.9% of the electorate. Only 99.9%, because 100% would look suspicious. It would look *ouya-ouya*.

Now that it had a new constitution, the country needed a civilian president. For six weeks Samuel Doe travelled to every district explaining how he'd become a civilian in word and deed. And on a different Sunday morning, in the presence of international observers, he was elected with 99.9% of the vote. Only 99.9%, because 100% would look *ouya-ouya*; it would set tongues wagging, ('tongues wagging' means people spreading malicious gossip.)

There he was, a top-notch, committed, respectable and respected president. His first concrete act as president was to relieve the malefactor Thomas Quionkpa of his duties, like a lowlife ('relieve of duty' means 'to remove from office, to strip an officer of his rank'). Relieve him of his duties, like a blackguard plotting a military coup. But that's when things went sour because Thomas Quionkpa wasn't going to let Doe walk all over him. No way!

With a bunch of other officers, Gio officers like himself, Thomas Quionkpa went off and plotted a real military coup. It was a narrow escape, a close call, the military coup almost succeeded. It was a narrow escape, a close call, Samuel Doe was almost assassinated. Well, after that, Samuel Doe got really angry because now he had the evidence he'd been looking for for a long time. He had Thomas Quionkpa horribly tortured and then he had him shot. His praetorian guard spread out across the city and assassinated almost all the Gio officers in the Republic of Liberia. And all their wives and all their children.

Now Samuel Doe was happy and triumphant, the one leader, surrounded only by officers from his own tribe, Krahn officers. The Republic of Liberia became a Krahn state, a hundred percent Krahn state. It didn't last long. Because luckily about thirty Gio officers escaped the assassins that were sent to assassinate them and fled to Côte d'Ivoire where they went begging to the dictator Houphouët-Boigny. Houphouët-Boigny was sympathetic and consoled them and sent them off to the dictator of Libya, Mister Qaddafi, who has lots of camps for training terrorists. For two whole years, Qaddafi trained the thirty Gio officers in arms drill and terrorism, and then he sent them back to Côte d'Ivoire, where the highly trained officers hid out in the villages on the border between Côte d'Ivoire and Liberia. They were very inconspicuous right up to the fateful day ('fateful' means 'destined to happen') 24 December 1989, Christmas Eve 1989. On Christmas Eve 1989, they waited until all the border guards at Boutoro (a border town) were dead drunk, a hundred percent drunk, then attacked them. They quickly overran the Boutoro border post, massacred the border guards and took all their guns. Now that the border guards were dead, the officers pretended to be the border guards and got on the phone and called army headquarters in Monrovia. They told headquarters that the border guards had fought off an attack and requested reinforcements. The army dispatched reinforcements. The reinforcements walked straight into an ambush, they were all massacred, all killed, all emasculated, and all their weapons were seized. The Gio officers, the rebels, had weapons, lots of weapons. That's why people say, why the historians say, that tribal wars arrived in Liberia on Christmas Eve 1989. The tribal wars started on 24 December 1989, exactly ten years to the day before the military coup in Côte d'Ivoire, the country next door. After 24 December 1989, Samuel Doe's problems would just proliferate until the day he died ('proliferate' means 'grow or multiply'). Proliferate until the day he was hacked to death. We'll get to that part later. I haven't got time at the moment. *Gnamokodé!*

Strangers were not welcome at ULIMO. That's the way it is with tribal wars. As soon as we arrived, we told the ULIMO people a story we'd made up all about Samuel Doe and his patriotism and his generosity. About all the good things he'd done for everyone in Liberia. About his sacrifice for his country. Etc. They listened to the story carefully, religiously, for a long time. After that, they asked us to hand over our guns. We handed over our guns with confidence. One of them brought out a Qur'an and a Bible and some grigris and made us swear on the holy books and the grigris. We solemnly swore that we were not thieves, that not a single one of us was a thief. Because ULIMO had more than enough thieves, they didn't need any more, they had them up to here. And then they banged us up in prison. Krik-krak.

The food in the prisons at ULIMO was very disgusting and there was very, very little of it. Yacouba was the first to complain about the terrible conditions. He shouted, 'I am a grigriman, a grigriman, I can make powerful grigris to protect people from whistling bullets.' But they didn't hear him. So he shouted even louder, 'Get me out of here. Otherwise I'll put a curse on you. I'll curse you all.' So then they came and got him and Yacouba said he wasn't going anywhere without me and asked if I could go with him.

They sent us to the headquarters of General Baclay – Onika Baclay Doe. Baclay was a woman. (You'd think it would be the feminine *Générale* but according to my *Larousse*, *Générale* is only used for a general's wife and never for a general who is a woman herself.) Anyway, they introduced us to General Onika Baclay Doe. General Baclay was happy to see Yacouba. She already had an animist grigriman but she didn't have a Muslim grigriman. Because of certain things that happened, she was starting to have doubts about the knowledge and the skill of her animist grigriman. With Yacouba, she had two grigrimen and that was so much the better.

I was sent off to the child-soldiers. They showed me my kalash. There were five of us to a gun and the one they showed me was newer than the one I had at the NPFL.

Child-soldiers were well looked after at ULIMO. You got lots to eat and you could even make money — dollars even — working as a bodyguard for the gold panners. I wanted to save some of my money, I didn't want to piss away everything I earned on drugs, like the other child-soldiers. With my savings, I bought gold and I kept the gold in one of the grigris that I wore. I wanted something to give my aunt when I finally got to meet her. *Faforo!*

General Baclay was weird, but she was a good woman and in her own way she was very fair: she shot men and women just the same, she shot thieves and it didn't matter if they stole a needle or a cow. A thief is a thief, and she shot every one of them. She was impartial.

General Baclay's capital, Sanniquellie, was a den of thieves. It was like every single thief in the Republic of Liberia had turned up at Sanniquellie. The child-soldiers knew all about it, because sometimes they got really stoned and crashed out and when they'd wake up they'd be naked, completely naked. The thieves took everything, even their underwear. They'd wake up lying naked next to their kalashes.

Any thieves that were caught red-handed during the week are arrested and chained up in prison. ('Red-handed' means they committed the crime right before the very eyes of the people who saw them committing it.) They might be hungry because of the laws of nature, but it was just too bad because in Baclay's jail the prisoners didn't get any food.

On Saturday mornings at about nine o'clock all the defendants are taken to the marketplace in chains and the whole population turns out. The trial takes place right there in front of everyone. The way it works is the defendant is asked if he is a thief, yes or no? If he says yes, he's condemned to death. If he says no, he is confounded by witnesses and then condemned to death anyway ('confound' means to silence someone by proving they committed the crime). So it's *kif-kif*, same difference. The accused are always condemned to death. And the guilty are taken to the place of execution straight away.

They're brought steaming rice with palm butter sauce and big hunks of meat and they pounce on it like wild beasts because they're so hungry, and it's so completely totally delicious that it makes some of the people watching wish they could swap places with the convicts. The convicts eat and eat for a long time. They eat till they're full, till they're stuffed. Then they say goodbye to their friends. It doesn't matter if the condemned man is Catholic or not, the chaplain goes round and gives everyone the last rites. Then they're tied to wooden stakes and they're blindfolded. Some of them cry like spoiled brats, but not too many of them cry. Most of them, the majority, lick their lips and burst out laughing. They laugh really loud on account of how they're so happy because of all the good food. Then they're shot dead, to the applause of the lively, cheerful crowd.

And in spite of everything, yes in spite of everything, some of the people watching are surprised to discover that, while they were clapping, thieves relieved them of their wallets because there are so many thieves in Sanniquellie that executing a bunch of them won't serve as a lesson to the rest. *Faforo!*

*　　*　　*

Onika was Samuel Doe's twin sister from an origin and kinship point of view. At the time of the indigenous military coup against the Afro-Americans she was a working girl. (For a girl, if you're working, it means you're a prostitute.) Back then she was called Onika Dokui. But as soon as her brother's military coup succeeded, he made her a sergeant in the Liberian army and she changed her name and started calling herself Baclay. Baclay because it sounded more Black Nigger Afro-American and, whatever people say, being Afro-American in Liberia gives you a certain amount of prestige. It's a lot better than being an indigene, being a Black Nigger African Native.

Back from Lomé after the CDEAO heads of state summit, Samuel Doe made Sergeant Baclay a lieutenant and posted her to his security staff. After the Gio military coup, Samuel Doe made her commander of the Presidential Guard. After Samuel Doe's death, after Samuel Doe was hacked to pieces, Baclay promoted herself to general and chief of Sanniquellie. So you can see that the general was a cunning woman who didn't let the sauce at the bottom of the *kanari* be licked up by *ouya-ouya* men. *Walahé!*

General Onika was a small woman, lively as a nanny-goat whose kid has been taken from her. With her general's stripes and her AK-47, she ran the whole show. She went everywhere in her four-by-four crammed with bodyguards armed to the teeth. The whole administration was a Baclay family thing. She left the day-to-day running of things to her son. Her son's name was Johnny Baclay Doe. He was a colonel and he commanded the most experienced regiment. The son had married three wives and all three wives were commanders in charge of the three most important subdivisions: finance, prisons and child-soldiers.

The wife in charge of the finances was called Sita. She was a Malinké, or a Mandingo in Afro-American pidgin. She collected the fees the gold panners had to pay every three months. She was Muslim, but she wasn't humanitarian at all. She thought that the gold panners who worked without permits were robbing the ground and every Saturday morning they were condemned to death. And then shot dead. And she'd stand there laughing.

Monita was the name of the commander in charge of the prisons. She was a Protestant and a humanitarian with a heart of gold. She gave food to the prisoners, even though they weren't allowed to eat. To prisoners who had only a couple of hours to live, she gave all the food they wanted. Allah is aware of acts like this and he rewards them in paradise.

The wife responsible for the child-soldiers was called Rita Baclay. Rita Baclay loved me like it's not allowed. She called me Yacouba's boy and the grigriman's son had everything he wanted and could do whatever he liked. Sometimes, mainly when Colonel Baclay was away, she'd bring me to her hut, and coddle me with little meals ('coddle' is when you love someone and look after them). I'd eat my fill and while I was eating she'd be saying stuff like 'Little Birahima, you're so handsome, so beautiful. Do you know you're beautiful? Do you know you're handsome?' And after I finished eating, she always asked me to take off my clothes. And I would.

She would stroke my *bangala* gently, gently, and I'd get a hard-on like a donkey.

'If Colonel Baclay saw us, he wouldn't be happy.'

'Don't be afraid, he's not here.'

She would kiss my *bangala* over and over and then she'd swallow it, like a snake swallowing a rat. She used my *bangala* like a little toothpick.

I left her house whistling, proud and happy. *Gnamokodé!*

Sanniquellie was a huge border town where they mined gold and diamonds. Even with all the tribal wars, foreign traders would venture as far as Sanniquellie lured by the cheap gold. Everyone in Sanniquellie was under General Baclay's orders. General Baclay had the power of life and death over everyone in Sanniquellie and she used it. And abused it.

Sanniquellie was made up of four districts. There was the native district and the district where the foreigners lived and between the two districts was the market. The market was only open on Saturdays after they executed thieves. At the other end of Sanniquellie, at the foot of a hill, was the refugee district and, on top of the hill, the military base where we lived. The military base had human skulls on stakes all round the boundary. In tribal wars that's really important. Far away, past the hills, out on the savannah were the river and the mines. The military base was guarded by child-soldiers. The mines and the river where the ore was washed were an unholy mess. I'm not going to describe them because I'm a street kid and I can do what I like, I don't give a fuck about anyone. But I will tell you about the bossman partners, who were really in charge of the money and all and everything.

The bossman partners are real chiefs and true masters. They live where they work and their living quarters are like fortresses guarded by child-soldiers armed to the teeth and permanently drugged up. Full of drugs from head to toe. Wherever there's child-soldiers, there's skulls on stakes. The bossman partners are rich. All the gold panners are accountable to one of the bossman partners.

When a gold panner starts out, he's usually got nothing except his underpants. The bossman is the one who pays for everything, for the hoes and the basket and the food. The bossman even pays the monthly charge, half an American dollar, for exploiting the land.

When the gold panner makes a find (that means if he's lucky enough to find a nugget of gold), he pays the bossman everything he owes. It doesn't happen too often because usually by the time the gold panner finds something valuable he's already up to his neck in debt to the bossman. That means he's always and permanently at the disposal of the bossman partner. A lot of the bossmen partners are Lebanese and it's easy to see why people are always murdering them. It's a good thing that lots of them get horribly murdered, because they're vampires. ('Vampire' means 'a person, such as an extortionist, who preys upon others', according to the *Petit Robert*.)

You should see what happens when a gold panner finds a nugget. It's worth the trip. There's this big hullabaloo, and the gold panner shouts for the child-soldiers to come and protect him, and the child-soldiers who are fucked up on drugs come running and surround the gold panner and take him to his bossman partner. Then the bossman partner calculates how much the gold panner owes, pays the taxes, pays the child-soldiers doing the protecting, and whatever is left over – if there's anything left over – goes to the gold panner. Now the gold panner is depressed on account of now he has to have a bodyguard until he's spent all his money, and obviously the bodyguard is one of the drugged-up child-soldiers. *Walahé!* A child-soldier needs drugs and hash doesn't grow on trees, it's expensive.

One night bandits armed to the teeth arrived in Sanniquellie. They used the darkness to sneak between the huts like thieves. They went to the sector where the bossman partners lived. They laid siege to two of the bossman partners' huts. It was easy, the child-soldiers were fucked up on drugs and so were the grown-up soldiers. The thieves took the bossman partners by surprise while they were sleeping. At machine-gun point they demanded that the bossman partners hand over the keys to their safes. The bossman partners handed over the keys. The thieves helped themselves, generously helped themselves. Just as they were leaving, they tried to kidnap the bossman partners but one of the bossman partners resisted and that's when all hell broke loose. One of the child-soldiers woke up and started shooting. That's all child-soldiers do, they just shoot and shoot. And that set off the riot. There was lots of furious gunfire and consequences: bodies, lots of dead bodies. *Walahé!* Five child-soldiers and three real soldiers got massacred. The safes were empty, empty from top to bottom, and the thieves fled with two of the bossman partners as hostages. You should have seen it! It was a terrible sight. There were corpses everywhere, soldiers and child-soldiers dead, safes empty and two bossmen missing. The dead child-soldiers weren't my friends, I didn't even know them, that's why I'm not doing a funeral oration for them. I'm not obliged to. *Gnamokodé!*

Onika Baclay arrived at the crime scene where everything happened. She couldn't hold back her tears. You should have seen it. It was worth the trip. A bitch like Onika crying over dead people. Crocodile tears! She wasn't crying over the corpses, she was crying over everything she had to lose.

You see, Onika was responsible for keeping the bossmen safe. No bossmen, no gold panners; no gold panners, no gold; and no gold meant no dollars. Onika guaranteed she could keep the bossmen safe – she was always boasting about it – and now two of the bossmen had been kidnapped, snatched in the middle of the night from their huts slap bang in the middle of Sanniquellie. All the other bossman partners wanted to leave, to shut up shop. Onika's whole system was falling apart.

Onika was like a madwoman. You should have seen it. This dumpy little woman, with everything she had to put up with, was shouting, 'Stay! Stay! I'll find them, I'll bring them back. They're in Niangbo. I know they are! They're in Niangbo! In Niangbo!'

This was the first time I'd heard her mention Niangbo; Niangbo was where my aunt lived. The thieves had come from Niangbo.

Two days after the kidnap, the ransom demand arrived. The kidnappers demanded ten thousand American dollars, and not one dollar less, for each of the bossman partners.

'It's too much, too much! Ten thousand dollars! Where am I going to find that kind of money? Where am I going to get my hands on that?' screamed General Onika.

Negotiations began without delay. Baclay offered two thousand dollars for each bossman. The bandits were sympathetic and asked for eight thousand dollars, but not a dollar less, and if they didn't get it they would slit the bossmen's throats.

Negotiations were long and difficult seeing as how Niangbo was a two-day walk from Sanniquellie.

Niangbo was a liberated town, a free town that didn't belong to any warlord factions. It had to remain neutral. It couldn't sanction kidnapping. But it did. It was a mistake and the inhabitants of Niangbo would pay. General Onika muttered constantly they would pay dearly.

While the negotiations were going on, General Onika was secretly planning to take Niangbo by force. Four days after the kidnapping, we, the child-soldiers, marched on Niangbo. We marched at night; during the day we stayed hidden in the jungle. To make sure we didn't fuck up along the way, we weren't given any supplies of hash and it got to where we were floppy as worms, weak on account of we needed hash. We were desperate, we didn't know what to do, we were just wandering round begging for a little bit of hash, but for the two days and two nights it took to get to Niangbo, the order was strictly enforced.

Now, here we are at last on a Sunday morning, happy that

we're finally on the outskirts of Niangbo. We made camp and they gave us masses of hash. We were the first ones to get there, the advance guard, the recon. We were dying to fight, we all felt as strong as bulls from all the hash and we all had faith in our grigris. Following behind, there was the platoon of real soldiers and, a bit farther back, General Onika's mobile headquarters. The operation was being supervised by the general herself. She was determined to be there to personally punish the people of Niangbo. She brought her grigriman with her, her two grigrimen, Yacouba and her old grigriman whose name was Sogou. Sogou was a grigriman of the Krahn tribe. Rain and shine, he wore a band of feathers around his head and his waist. His body was painted with kaolin.

The assault began at dawn. We had crept as far as the first huts. Every AK-47 was manned by five child-soldiers. The first group attacked and to our surprise our first bursts of gunfire were answered by their bursts of gunfire. The people and the soldiers of Niangbo had been expecting us. There was no element of surprise. The kid manning the kalash fell down dead and another kid took over, then he fell down dead too. Then it was the third kid's turn. When it came to the fourth one, he refused and we retreated, leaving our dead on the battlefield. General Onika's entire strategy was in jeopardy. Grown-up soldiers went to the front line and brought back the bodies of the dead.

The child-soldiers — that's us — had to go to the headquarters to have our protective grigris tested. We must have done something terrible that made the grigris ineffective: three dead in the first exchange of fire. When Yacouba had tested the grigris, he told us that the child-soldiers had violated the taboos attached to the grigris. We had violated the taboos by smoking hash. Smoking hash is a taboo during wartime when you're wearing war grigris. I was so angry I went red in the face. Well, no . . . on account of blacks like me don't go red when they're angry, that's only for whites. Blacks get hot and bothered. I was hot and bothered I was so angry, I was furious. Grigrimen are charlatans. ('Charlatan' means 'a quack or fraud who makes elaborate claims to skill or knowledge', according to my *Larousse*.) It's the truth! According to the grigriman, three kids were dead just because we smoked hash. Coming out with bullshit like that. It was unbelievable!

I cried for their mothers. I cried for all the life they never lived. Among the bodies, I recognised Sekou the Terrible.

It was school fees that had done for Sekou Ouedroago. It was school fees that had thrown him into the jaws of the alligator, into the ranks of child-soldiers.

Sekou's father was a security guard at one of the luxury villas over in Deux Plateaux somewhere in Abidjan. When thieves broke into the prosperous man's house, he accused Sekou's father of being involved. Seeing as how there's no justice for the poor man on this earth, Sekou's father was sent to prison. For one month, two months, Sekou's school fees didn't get paid . . . After three months, the headmaster sent for Sekou and said, 'Sekou, you're suspended. You can come back when your fees are paid.'

Sekou's mother was called Bita. Bita said to her son, 'Wait

there, I'll raise the money, I'll get you the school fees.' Bita sold cooked rice, and some of the building workers she sold to owed her fifteen thousand CFA francs. With fifteen thousand CFA francs, she would have enough to pay the monthly fees of five thousand francs. Sekou waited a whole week, then another whole week, but when there was no sign of any money Sekou thought about his uncle in Burkina Faso. His father had often told him that Boukari, one of his brothers, one of Sekou's uncles, was a driver who had his own car and his own house in Ouagadougou. Sekou decided to go and ask his uncle with the car and the house in Ouagadougou for the school fees. He jumped a train (to 'jump a train' means you don't pay the fare), but when he got to Ouagadougou he was arrested and sent to the Ouagadougou police headquarters.

'Where are your parents?'

'My uncle's name is Boukari, he's got a car and a house.'

But finding a Boukari with a car and a house in a place as huge as Ouagadougou is like looking for a grain of millet with a black spot on it in a huge sack of millet. Sekou stayed in the police station for a week, waiting for the police to find his uncle. The second week, while the search was still going on, Sekou took advantage when the guard was distracted and escaped into big old Ouagadougou. He roamed around big old Ouagadougou. During his wanderings, he spotted a truck from Abidjan. There was nobody but the driver: his apprentice, his boy, had quit because the driver didn't pay him. Sekou was quick to introduce himself as a kid who would work hard for no money. It was a done deal, the driver, whose name was Mamadou, hired Sekou to be his new boy. Mamadou took Sekou behind the truck and in a low voice explained their mission. It was a very secret top-secret mission and Sekou was not allowed to breathe a word about it to anyone, ever. The truck wasn't going to Abidjan at all, the truck was being used to secretly transport arms to the Taylor faction in Liberia.

The very same night, soldiers in civvies showed up ('civvies' are civilian clothes or normal clothes). The soldiers rented a hotel room for Mamadou and Sekou while they headed off to load up the truck. They came back to the hotel at four o'clock in the morning with the truck fully loaded. The shipment was completely disguised. The soldiers woke Mamadou and Sekou. One of the officers in civvies sat up front in the cab next to Mamadou and another one, also in civvies, perched next to Sekou on all the disguised crates. They headed for the Liberian/Ivoirian border. As soon as they got there, guer-rillas – rebel fighters – appeared out of the forest. One guer-rilla took over the driving from Mamadou and three got in the back of the truck with the cargo. They drove off with the officers while Sekou and Mamadou were invited to wait in a *maquis*, an illegal bar where rebels meet.

The owner of the bar was an alcoholic and a really funny guy. He was always laughing and slapping his customers on the back and farting all the time. While he was clowning around, four guys in balaclavas appeared out of the forest (a balaclava is like a hood but with a hole where your eyes are). They pointed a gun on Sekou and Mamadou, but before they kidnapped them they gave a message to the owner of the *maquis*, who was standing there shaking like a leaf.

'We're taking them hostage, the ransom is five million CFA francs to be paid by the government of Burkina Faso within five days. Otherwise, the hostages' heads will come back on stakes. Understand?'

'Yes,' answered the bar owner, still trembling.

Blindfolded, Sekou and Mamadou were led through the forest to a *paillote*, a small straw hut, where they were tied to stakes. For the first three days, there were three guards who always seemed on the alert. By the fourth day, there was only one guard left and he fell asleep. Sekou and Mamadou managed to untie themselves and disappear into the forest. From the forest, Sekou emerged on to a road. It was a straight road. He walked along the road, not looking right or left. At the end of the road, there was a village and in the village there were child-soldiers. He went right up to the head of the organisation and said, 'My name is Sekou Ouedraogo, I want to be a child-soldier.'

What Sekou did to earn his nickname 'Sekou the Terrible' is a different story, it's a long story. I don't feel like telling it and I'm not obliged to, and anyway it makes me sad, really sad. When I saw Sekou lying there all dead like that, I cried my heart out. And this had all happened, according to the lying bastard grigrimen, because of the hash. *Faforo!*

Next to Sekou was the body of Sosso the Panther.

Sosso the Panther was a kid from the village of Salala in Liberia. He had a mother and a father. His father was a security guard and a labourer in a shop owned by a Lebanese man. Sosso's father did all the work and more and every night he got drunk mainly on whisky and lots of palm wine a go-go. Every night Sosso's father came home drunk, so drunk he couldn't tell his wife from his son. Every evening, as soon as the sun started to set, Sosso and his mother started trembling because the master of the house was coming home drunk, completely drunk, so drunk he couldn't tell a bull from a billy-goat. And they were going to get what was coming to them.

One night, they heard him in the distance, heard him in the distance singing and laughing and blaspheming (to 'blaspheme' is to say rude things about God). Sosso and his maman thought about what was coming and went and hid in the kitchen. When he got home and there was no sign of his wife and his son, Sosso's father got even angrier and started smashing everything. Sosso's mother came out of the kitchen trembling and crying and begging him to stop the massacre, but his father threw a cooking pot at her and she started bleeding. In tears, Sosso grabbed a kitchen knife and stabbed his father who howled like a hyena and died.

The only thing left for Sosso the Parricide (a 'parricide' is a boy who kills his father) was to join the child-soldiers.

When you haven't got no father, no mother, no brothers, no sisters, no aunts, no uncles, when you haven't got nothing at all, the best thing to do is become a child-soldier. Being a child-soldier is for kids who've got fuck all left on earth or Allah's heaven.

What Sosso did to earn the nickname 'Sosso the Panther' is a different story, it's a long story. I don't feel like telling it and I'm not obliged to, and anyway it makes me sad, really sad. When I saw Sosso lying there all dead like that, I cried my heart out. And when I thought about the bullshit grigrimen saying it was all on account of us smoking hash at the wrong time it made me even angrier. *Faforo!*

We buried them all in a mass grave. When the grave had been filled, we fired our kalashes. There's no funeral orations when you're on the front line.

Onika believed the grigrimen a hundred percent when they said that the three child-soldiers got massacred on account of smoking hash at the wrong time. The grigris of the child-soldiers needed to be re-energised. The ceremony had to be done on the bank of a river, and choosing the river was no easy thing because if one of the grigrimen said one thing the other grigriman disagreed. Onika was forced to shout and make threats before the shaman grigriman and the Muslim grigriman would agree.

Onika arrived with her son and her daughters-in-law and the rest of the members of the high command stood around them. The child-soldiers were brought out, all of the child-soldiers, about thirty of us. Me and some of my friends didn't believe the grigrimen's bullshit and we were laughing up our sleeves the whole time during the recharging ('laugh up your sleeve' means 'laugh or rejoice in secret at another's error', according to *Larousse*). They lined us all up, then, one after another, they made all of us recite a short prayer:

spirits of the ancestors, spirit of each and every ancestor.
Spirits of water, spirits of forest, spirits of mountain, spirits of
nature all, humbly I confess that I have sinned.

Day and night I ask your forgiveness, I smoked hash in time of war.

We took off our grigris and put them in a pile. The pile was set alight, and the flames reduced its prey to ashes. The ashes were scattered on the water.

Then all the child-soldiers got naked, completely naked. It wasn't very discreet seeing as how there were women there. There was Sita Baclay, Monita Baclay and Rita Baclay. When Rita saw us naked, when she saw me naked, it made her think about the lovely times we'd spent together. *Walahé!*

The grigrimen passed down the line of child-soldiers, spat on the head of each of them, and rubbed the spit into our heads. Then the order was given for the child-soldiers to jump into the river. Which they did cheerfully, shouting and mucking around. After they'd jumped into the water and made a racket, the order was given to get out of the water. The child-soldiers all got out on the right bank of the river. They dried themselves off and – still naked – walked down the river to a small bridge by which they crossed back to the left bank, where they had left their clothes and their guns. They got dressed and lined up again. Me and some of my friends who didn't believe in their bullshit grigris laughed up our sleeves. *Gnamokodé!*

All this took twenty-four hours. We fooled the people of Niangbo into thinking we'd taken our dead and left, disappeared into the forest. Then in the morning, really early in the morning, there was another free-for-all. There was tons of gunfire, but we still didn't surprise them. *Tat-tat-tat*, they fired right back at us with long bursts of machine-gun fire. There we were again, lying flat on the ground. Two soldiers got shot in spite of all the bullshit Muslim grigris and shaman grigris. The first soldier was killed dead and the second was fatally wounded. No child-soldiers were killed this time, seeing as how the child-soldiers weren't in the front line. Even though we attacked was from the south, near the river, not north of the village like the first time. They'd obviously put soldiers with kalashes all the way round the village. There we were again, lying on our bellies.

We needed a different strategy, something other than the bullshit grigris, but instead of racking her brains for a stratagem, Onika just sent for the bullshit grigrimen again. They gathered together some of the soldiers and a few child-soldiers including Tête Brûlée to talk about strategy. The meeting went on till it was dark.

Then, suddenly, armed with lots of grigri necklaces, his kalash in his fist, Tête Brûlée marched straight towards the village. He kept advancing, machine-gunning like a madman, machine-gunning relentlessly, ('relentlessly' means 'without stopping'), machine-gunning like ten men. Relentlessly, ignoring all the bullets from the soldiers on the other side who countered machine-gun with machine-gun. You should have seen it. *Walahé!* He walked into the machine-gun fire with such balls, with so much balls between his legs, that the machine-gunners on the other side retreated. Backed away. They were so scared they dropped their guns and ran.

That's just what we had been waiting for. We all roared

and rushed towards the huts. And to our total surprise, terrified villagers came out of the huts with their hands up waving white flags. All over the village all the inhabitants came out with their hands up, waving the white flag.

Tête Brûlée, with his courage and his grigris, had conquered the village of Niangbo. When the soldiers saw Tête Brûlée walking into the machine-gun fire, they knew Tête Brûlée's grigris were stronger than theirs so they panicked and threw down their guns.

It was about this time that I realised I didn't understand this fucking universe, I didn't understand a thing about this bloody world, I couldn't make head or tail of people or society. Tête Brûlée with his grigris had just taken Niangbo! Was this grigri bullshit true or not true? Who was there who could tell me? Where could I go to find out? Nowhere. Maybe this grigri thing is true . . . or maybe it's a lie, a scam, a con that runs the whole length and breadth of Africa. *Faforo!*

The town of Niangbo had been taken by four rebel bandits, the same four thieves that had kidnapped the bossman partners in Sanniquellie. They locked up the village chief and all the important people in Niangbo and then the four of them had stationed themselves at the four cardinal points of the town. They were the ones who had killed the child-soldiers. As soon as they'd legged it into the forest, all the villagers came out of their huts.

They organised celebrations. We were their liberators. On the village square the dancing was getting wilder.

You should have seen that bitch Onika play the liberator. It was worth the trip! There she was, sitting in the middle of everything with her son and her daughters-in-law on either side, lording it over everyone like a nabob, a mogul. The tamtam player came towards her, bowed down at her feet, and played in her honour. Right then, Onika let out a wild cry and threw herself into the circle of dancers, still wearing the stripes, the kalash, the grigris, the whole works. Her son and her daughters-in-law followed, followed her into the circle of the dance. The women lifted Onika's arms into the air, two to each arm. Everyone started clapping like mad, singing and laughing like lunatics. The daughters-in-law and the son left Onika in the middle of the circle. She started the monkey dance. You should have seen that arsehole Onika jumping around like a monkey, turning somersaults like a street kid in her general's stripes. She was drunk, totally and absolutely pissed. She was so happy, so proud of her victory. She was drunk on palm wine.

After her turn in the circle, she came and sat with her daughters-in-law and her son. They kissed her on the mouth. The clamour stopped. And Onika spoke.

She had her two grigrimen, Yacouba and Sogou, brought into the circle where she publicly congratulated them. Only through their wisdom had Niangbo been taken without much loss of life. The grigrimen were proud and happy. They walked round the circle fiddling with their grigris.

She had the two bossman partners who had been kidnapped brought into the circle. Onika told everyone why the kidnappers had not been able to kill the bossmen — it was on account of the grigris and the sacrifices! She kept on speechi-fying. The four thieves who had taken the town of Niangbo would be hunted down and arrested. Then they would be hacked limb from limb and bits of their bodies would be exhibited in every place they had committed their crimes to appease the wrath of the grigris. Soldiers were already hunting them. Eventually, they would capture them. Absolutely, *inchallah*, God willing . . . Amen!

Suddenly, two Mandingos in filthy *bubus* went up to Yacouba and shouted loud so as to get everyone's attention.

'You – I know. You before in Abidjan, you truck driver, you money-multiplier, healer, you many things. *Walahé!* Me know you, you name Yacouba . . .'

'Bastard! Fool!' Yacouba responded. He didn't let the man say any more. 'You shout so loud, everyone will hear.' He took him aside and said, 'If you recognise me again you don't need to shout it from the rooftops. Onika will hear and that is not good for me.'

Yacouba did not want Onika to know everything he'd got up to in his bullshit life.

Then Yacouba realised that one of the Mandingos was his friend Sekou. Sekou who had come to visit him in his Mercedes Benz at the Yopougon teaching hospital in Abidjan. He was so scrawny that Yacouba hadn't recognised him. Yacouba and Sekou kissed each other and reeled off the miles and miles of greetings Dioulas come out with every time they meet: 'How's your brother's sister-in-law's cousin?' etc.

After a minute of silence, Sekou and his companion started

talking about the people from their village who had landed up in fucked-up Liberia, and Sekou's friend mentioned Mahan and her husband.

'Mahan is my aunt,' I shouted.

I tell you, right then, Sekou's friend and me both started like hyenas caught stealing a goat.

'Mahan! Mahan!' cried Yacouba pointing at me. 'She his aunt, Mahan this boy aunt, I look for her. Where she live? She live where?'

And we started rushing around like lunatics, like we all had diarrhoea. You should have seen Yacouba the crippled crook running round. We searched concession after concession, hut after hut. There were corpses outside some of the huts, all kinds of corpses, some had their eyes open like badly slaughtered pigs. We searched the huts to the north and the huts to the south until we were tired . . . Then we started to get demoralised. ('Demoralised' means your heart's not in it any more, you don't want to do fuck all any more.) We were standing there watching the flies flying over and back, not saying anything. Suddenly, Sekou's friend stopped, leaned forward, then turned into a yard in front of a hut and roared like a bull, '*Walahé! Walahé!* This Mahan hut. Mahan inside here.'

The door was half-open. Yacouba pushed. There was nothing in the hut. We went out to the backyard, and there – *gnamokodé* – there was a dead body thick with flies bigger than bees. The flies flew off with a drone like a low-flying plane, leaving the bloody body all exposed. Terrifically smashed up, the skull crushed, the tongue ripped out, the genitals delicately sliced off. It was – *faforo!* – the body of my aunt Mahan's husband. We stopped dead and started to cry like little kids who'd pissed the bed again. There we were crying like a bunch of total arseholes when a man comes out of the hut and comes towards us. The man was a native, a Black Nigger African Native. He was trembling like a leaf in a storm.

'Krahns did this,' he said. 'They don't like the Mandingos. They don't want Mandingos here in Liberia. The Krahns came. They smashed his head; they ripped out his tongue and cut off his cock. His tongue and his prick, to make their grigris stronger. His wife, gentle Mahan, she saw them do this, quickly she ran and hid in my hut. When the Krahns had left, positively left, I took her to the edge of the forest. Quickly she ran off into the jungle. Ran to the south . . . She is so kind, so gentle, Mahan.'

And the guy started sobbing too.

'Where, where did she go?' shouted Yacouba, ready to jump up and run after her.

'Two days she is gone. You will not catch her; you will never find her now.'

We stood there flabbergasted ('flabbergasted' means 'overcome with astonishment'). Totally demoralised. Things weren't going well for my aunt: she was in deadly peril.

We went back to the square where a while ago people had been somersaulting and dancing like monkeys. Surprise! The party was over. It was total bedlam, chaos. Screaming and swearing and people going berserk.

Onika had just found out that the NPFL had taken advantage of her absence to launch an attack on Sanniquellie.

It was a piece of cake, they seized the camp and all the loot without firing a shot ('a piece of cake' means it was easy). No problem, no resistance, they just marched right into Sanniquellie and now they were in complete control. Onika was like a madwoman. The tiny woman was coming and going and screaming and swearing and ordering people around with her stripes and her kalash and her grigris, the whole works.

The NPFL had wanted to seize the gold-mining town of Sanniquellie for ages. They'd attacked several times, but every time they were driven back with lots of casualties.

'And now they exploit my absence with this trickery. They are spineless! NPFL are cowards. They are not men, they are gutless cowards!' screamed Onika.

What could Onika do now? Her headquarters was under enemy control, her organisation was leaderless, she had no guns, no army except the small detachment she had brought for the Niangbo operation. With all the arsenal in Sanniquellie, the NPFL had mounted a fearsome defence. All Onika's possessions, all her gold, had fallen into enemy hands.

Onika withdrew, sat down, her son and her daughters-in-law rallied round her. Soldiers, child-soldiers, joined them. Everyone huddled together, got into a circle, it was an organised concert of weeping. Everyone started sobbing. There we were, a bunch of criminals, crooks of the worse kind, crying like babies. You should have seen it, it was worth the trip.

After a long half-day of blubbering, everyone was hungry, everyone was thirsty. They pulled themselves together and sat down. The little army lined up in two rows with Onika leading the way and set off, foot to the road, heading north to find ULIMO. That's where ULIMO were, loads of them.

But we (we means Yacouba, the crippled crook, and me, the street kid) headed south. That's the way my aunt Mahan went. All we've got for subsistence is our kalashes, on account of how Allah never leaves empty a mouth he has created.

Today, 25 September 199 . . . I've had enough. I'm fed up telling my life story, with piling up dictionaries. I've had it up to here with everything. Fuck off, the lot of you. I'm shutting up now, I'm not saying another word today . . . *Gnamokodé! Faforo!*

4

We (we means Yacouba, the crippled crook, money-multiplier, Muslim grigriman, and me Birahima, the fearless, blameless street kid, the small-soldier) were heading south when we met our friend Sekou carrying a bundle on his head. We had parted company in Niangbo without saying our goodbyes. We were like Dioulas meeting in the forests of Liberia, greetings and more greetings, we reeled off miles of greetings. And when we got to the last of the last of the greetings, Sekou said something wonderful. Everyone in the universe was sick and tired of watching the Black Nigger African Natives of Liberia slaughtering each other like wild beasts drunk on blood. The whole world was sick and tired of watching the warlords who'd carved Liberia up between them committing atrocities ('atrocity' means 'an appalling or atrocious crime'). All the people in all the countries all over the world were sick and tired of the warlords getting away with it and they wanted it stopped. So all the countries got together and went to see the UN and the UN asked the CDEAO to intervene. The CDEAO asked Nigeria to do humanitarian peacekeeping. ('Humanitarian peacekeeping' is when one country is allowed to send soldiers into another country to kill innocent victims in their own country, in their own villages, in their own huts, sitting on their own mats.) Nigeria is the most heavily populated country in Africa and has loads of soldiers they don't know what to do with, so they sent their spare soldiers to Liberia with the right to massacre the innocent civilian population, the whole works. The Nigerian troops were known as the ECOMOG peace-keeping force. ECOMOG troops were now operating all over Liberia and even Sierra Leone and massacring people, all in the name of humanitarian peacekeeping. Apparently this is to create a buffer between rival factions.

Again we said goodbye to Sekou, the informant, thanked him and left him. We hadn't walked far, not even a whole day, when we got to a camp controlled by supporters of Prince Johnson. There were human skulls on stakes all around the border of the camp, like all military barracks in the tribal wars.

Prince Johnson was the third big important rebel warlord. He had exclusive rights over large parts of Liberia. But he was a prince, meaning he was a nice warlord because he had principles. Oh, yes, wonderful principles. Because Prince Johnson was a man of the Church, a warlord with his head stuffed full of incredible lordly principles, the principles of an honest, disinterested freedom fighter. He had made a law that any warlord who liberated Liberia with a gun in his hand could not stand for election. It would be against ethics ('ethics', according to the *Petit Robert*, means 'the rules or standards governing a person, morality'); it would be against decency ('decency', according to the *Petit Robert*, means 'the quality of conforming to standards of propriety and morality'). Prince Johnson's head full of principles had another lordly principle: a soldier does not loot, does not steal, but asks local people for food to eat. The craziest thing (I bet you won't believe this!) is that he even puts his principles into practice. *Walahé!*

Prince Johnson's principles mean that every guerrilla who arrived at his camp is locked up and stays locked up: and he's forced to swear that he will fight to the death any warlord who tries to present himself for election by universal suffrage; any warlord who tries to be president; any warlord who wants to rule independent Liberia, the beloved mother country.

Yacouba and me were locked up for a week, in appalling conditions. After a week, we made the bullshit speech, because it didn't mean we're obliged. Nobody can be obliged to do anything because no one's got the time to go round putting rebel fighters on trial for perjury in the fucked-up four-star chaos of tribal wars in Liberia ('perjury', according to my *Larousse*, means 'the deliberate, wilful giving of false testimony under oath'). After they've given false testimony, every new arrival is tested, over and over and over by the grigrimen. He has to get naked as the day he was born and then he's hosed down with some decoction. The decoction stinks of piss. Then a grigri and a cross are spun around his head. Two bearers snatch the grigri. Round the bearer's neck hangs a huge crucifix with a dying Jesus on it. The bearer shudders and twitches and a lot of other stuff like that. And for what? To make sure the new arrival isn't a devourer of souls. Prince Johnson didn't need any soul-eaters, he already had too many of them in his district. It was a haven for soul-eaters. (Black Nigger African Natives claim that at night Black Africans turn into owls and take the souls of their nearest and dearest and go off and devour them in the branches of the great kapok trees, the tallest trees in the village. That's the definition of devourer of souls, according to the *Glossary*.)

Yacouba and me got through all the tests and, luckily, we didn't give them any misgivings about maybe being devourers of souls ('misgiving' means 'a harmful doubt, real or imagined'). Because soul-eaters are beaten up and thrown out and locked up and tortured until they vomit up the knot of blood that every soul-eater has inside him. And I tell you, it's not easy, it's no easy thing for a devourer of souls to vomit up the knot of blood. He has to be whipped like a thieving dog and administered enough vomitive decoctions to give two horses diarrhoea (for Black Nigger African Natives who don't know too much, 'administer' means to give someone medicine).

When Yacouba introduced himself as a big important grigriman, Johnson said a short pious Christian prayer and ended with: 'May Jesus Christ and the Holy Spirit ensure that your grigris are always effective.' Johnson was a devout Christian.

Yacouba replied, '*Chi Allah la ho*, they will be.' (According to the *Glossary*, '*Chi Allah la ho*' means 'if Allah so wills'.) He, Yacouba, was a devout Muslim.

Johnson had a grigriman – a Christian grigriman. The grigriman's incantations always contained passages from the Bible and he always had a crucifix around somewhere ('incantation' means 'a formula used in ritual recitation; a verbal charm or spell'). Johnson was happy to meet Yacouba, a Muslim grigriman. He had never met a Muslim before. Now his guerrillas would be able to add grigris with verses from the Qur'an scrawled in Arabic to their Christian grigris.

Straight off, I was posted to the brigade of child-soldiers, small-soldiers, soldier-children with a kalash and a Para uniform that was too big for me. But the food was terrible, I mean really terrible. Nothing but boiled cassava and not even enough of that. Straight away, I tried to come up with a solution. I started by making loads of friends. Me and my friends were pretty resourceful. We stole food, we pilfered food. Pilfering food isn't stealing because Allah, Allah in his inordinate goodness, never intended to leave empty for two whole days a mouth he created. *Walahé!*

Prince Johnson was a seer, a visionary. And you don't argue with a visionary. You don't take the words of a visionary at face value, you don't unquestioningly believe what he says or promises. This is something Samuel Doe, the dictator, didn't realise until it was too late. Far too late! He only realised it when he saw, saw with his own two eyes, saw in his own lifetime, saw his limbs being hacked off bit by bit, piece by piece. Like the parts of an old car you're trying to fix.

Walahé! It was at noon, exactly at noon, that an ECOMOG officer showed up at Johnson's camp, Johnson's sanctuary in Monrovia. Prince Johnson was busy in prayer and penitence like he was every day at noon. He knelt on stones to pray, his knees were black and blue from the stones. He was in agony.

The officer announced that Samuel Doe in person was at ECOMOG headquarters, right downtown in the centre of Monrovia. ECOMOG headquarters was neutral territory where warlords had to hand over their weapons before going inside. Samuel Doe had gone to ECOMOG headquarters by himself with no guns and ninety bodyguards who had no guns either, they were all empty-handed and powerless. Samuel Doe had gone into ECOMOG headquarters to ask the commanding officer to act as intermediary between him, Samuel Doe, and Prince Johnson. He asked one thing, only one thing of Johnson: a chance to talk. Because Liberia was weary of her children fighting. Now that Johnson had broken off relations with Taylor, Samuel Doe and Johnson could be friends. Doe wanted to negotiate with Johnson an end to the war in Liberia. The war had done great harm to the beloved mother country.

Johnson shouted, 'Jesus Christ the Lord! Jesus Christ the Lord!' He licked his lips. He couldn't believe it, he couldn't believe Samuel Doe in person was at ECOMOG head-quarters. He gave thanks to Jesus Christ and all his saints. After a minute, he calmed down and spoke to the ECOMOG officer in the same kind of language Samuel Doe had used. He, Prince Johnson, was also weary of war. Samuel Doe was a patriot, and he, Prince Johnson, respected the patriot's gesture. Prince Johnson would go to ECOMOG and kiss him, kiss him right on the mouth like a friend. In private, as friends and patriots, they could discuss the affairs of the dearly beloved and blessed mother country Liberia. And so on.

He told the officer to go on ahead, go back to ECOMOG headquarters and inform Samuel Doe of Johnson's tribute. The officer did what he was told and Samuel Doe listened to these honeyed words and believed them. Calmly, smoking a cigarette, sitting in an armchair at ECOMOG headquarters, he waited for Johnson.

As soon as the officer turned his back, Johnson burst out laughing, laughing uncontrollably and muttering to himself. Here was a man who had gravely wronged the people of Liberia, a man of the devil. There he was, unarmed, in the centre of Monrovia. He, Prince Johnson, was a man of the Church, a man who had become involved in tribal wars at God's command. God had commanded that he, Prince Johnson, wage tribal war. Wage tribal war to kill the devil's men. The devil's men who had so gravely wronged the people of Liberia. And chief among the devil's men was Samuel Doe. Now God in his infinite goodness had offered Johnson a once-in-a-lifetime opportunity to take care of Samuel Doe once and for all. The voice of the Lord compelled him, it urged him on.

Prince Johnson organised a commando team of veteran

soldiers twenty men strong. He himself commanded the commandos. They hid their weapons under the seats of the Jeep. The guns were well hidden; they drove right past the checkpoint where visitors were supposed to hand in their weapons. As soon as they got inside the ECOMOG compound, they took out their guns and started massacring Samuel Doe's ninety bodyguards, then they went up to the first floor where Samuel Doe was meeting with the Ghanaian general who was in command of ECOMOG. The commando squad forced everyone to lie down, and they seized Samuel Doe. They tied Samuel Doe's hands behind his back, shoved him down the stairs, and threw him into a Jeep full of soldiers armed to the teeth. All of this was done double quick, at the double so that the ECOMOG forces had no time to regroup, to retaliate. The commando team was able to drive right out the gates of ECOMOG without firing a shot. The commandos brought Samuel Doe to the safety of Johnson's sanctuary ('sanctuary' means 'a secret, sacred place'). There, they untied him and threw him to the ground.

Once on the ground, in a fury of shoes and fists, in a fit of delirious laughter, Prince Johnson hurled himself at Samuel Doe screaming, 'You are the president of Liberia making war to remain president. You are a man of the devil! A man guided by the devil. You want to remain president by force of arms. President of the Republic, President of all the peoples of Liberia. Lord Jesus!'

He took Doe by the ear and sat him down. He cut off his ears, the right ear after the left.

'You want to negotiate with me. This is how I negotiate with the devil's minions.'

The more the blood flowed, the more Johnson laughed, the more delirious he became. Prince Johnson ordered that Samuel Doe's fingers be cut off, one by one, and, with his torture victim squealing like a suckling calf, he had his tongue cut out. Through the torrent of blood, Johnson hacked at the arms, one after the other. When he tried to hack off the left arm, the victim had had enough: he gave up the ghost ('give up the ghost' means 'die').

It was then, only then, that ECOMOG officers arrived at Johnson's camp. They had rushed there to negotiate the release of Samuel Doe. They arrived too late. They noted the torture and witnessed what followed ('torture' is corporal punishment that is enforced by justice).

Between wild fits of laughter, Johnson shouted orders. Samuel Doe's heart was removed. One of the officers ate some human flesh to make himself look more cruel, more brutal, more barbarous and inhuman – real, genuine human flesh. Samuel Doe's heart was put to one side for the officer so he could make a delicious kebab out of it. Then a tall rickety platform was set up outside the town on the road down there that leads to the cemetery. The dictator's carcass was lugged there and thrown on top of the platform. For two days and two nights it was left there, exposed to the vultures, until a royal vulture, majestically, came to perform the final act, came to pluck out the eyes, both eyes from their sockets. In doing so the royal vulture destroyed Samuel Doe's immanent power and the immanent forces of his many grigris. ('Immanent' is that which is inherent, which comes from the very nature of the thing itself.)

After that, the carcass, whose stench could be smelled a mile away, was taken down and thrown to a pack of dogs. A pack of overexcited dogs that fought it out, snarling and biting for two days and two nights under the platform. The dogs attacked the corpse, wolfed it down, carved it up between them. They made a hearty meal of it, a tasty lunch.

Faforo! Gnamokodé!

Mother Superior Marie-Béatrice was a saint who made love like every woman in the universe. Except it was hard to imagine the saint underneath a man receiving love on account of how she was a virago. (A 'virago' is a woman whose looks and manner are masculine.) She was too muscular and too tall. She had a wide, spreading nose, her lips were too thick and she had the eyebrows of a gorilla. And another thing: her hair was cropped short. And another thing: she had rolls of fat at the back of her head like men have. And another thing: she wore a soutane. And another thing: on top of the soutane she wore a kalash. And all that was on account of tribal wars. But it was really, honestly, hard to imagine her kissing Prince Johnson on the lips and lying underneath him to take his love. *Walahé!*

Let's start at the start.

When the tribal wars arrived in Monrovia, Marie-Béatrice was mother superior of the biggest convent school in the capital. The bishop's palace sent ten soldiers and eighteen child-soldiers under the command of a captain to defend the school. The captain deployed his men. And then looters came along and attacked the convent. The guards panicked and were quickly outmanoeuvred. The looters started to loot all the holy relics. Well, that got Saint Marie-Béatrice really angry, she took off her cornet, ripped a kalash out of one of the soldiers' hands, got down on the ground, and machine-gunned and machine-gunned. She killed five looters and the rest of them made a run for it. From then on, Saint Marie-Béatrice took the defence of the convent in hand, in her iron fist. She informed the captain that he and his men were to take orders from her and her alone.

Before attacking the convent school, the looters had taken the bishop's palace where they horribly tortured the monsignor and five priests before murdering them. The rest of them ran away, made off like thieves. Marie-Béatrice's convent school was the only institution still functioning in the centre of Monrovia, seeing as how all the other Catholic missions and all the houses round the convent school had been looted, and abandoned by their occupants. That's where Marie-Béatrice showed herself equal to the challenge; that's when she performed her miracles, her feats, her acts of heroism; that's when she earned her stripes as an actual, genuine saint.

For Saint Marie-Béatrice, every day was the same, each one just twenty-four hours long and it never seemed enough. Every day there was always work left over for the saint to do the next day. Marie-Béatrice woke up at four in the morning, grabbed the kalash that she always had right by her side all night. That's tribal wars for you. She put on her cornet, her soutane, tied her shoelaces and then quietly crept up to the sentry posts to surprise the sentries. Every morning she surprised the stupid sentries snoring and kicked them in the arse to wake them up, then she'd come back inside and ring the bell. The nuns and everyone else in the convent woke up for morning prayers. After that, there was breakfast if last night's alms had been plentiful ('alms' means 'money or food given as charity to the poor').

Saint Marie-Béatrice would have her four-by-four convertible brought round, and she'd sit up front beside the driver wearing her kalash and her cornet, obviously. She'd arrive back at about ten or eleven and every day, she performed the same miracle, because the four-by-four would arrive stuffed with victuals ('victuals' means 'provisions, food'). Then she'd start the healing. The crippled, the lame, the blind would gather round her and she would heal them vigorously. Then she would go into the courtyard where there were sick people all over the place, some even lying on the ground ready to drop dead, and the nuns would tend to them and Saint Marie-Béatrice would give them the last rites. After that, she would do a quick tour of the kitchen and she'd always find little brats dodging in and out between the cooks pilfering vegetables and eating them raw. She'd give them a whack of her stick like you'd give a thieving dog. They screamed and ran away.

Then came lunch; but before that Saint Marie-Béatrice would thank the Good Lord for giving them their daily bread. After lunch came religious education. Everyone listened to the religious education, even the cripples and the blind and the people about to drop dead. Then there was more healing on account of there was always a couple of the sick who needed to be healed twice a day. Then there was dinner if last night's alms had been plentiful and after that came the interminable evening prayer. Before she went to bed, Saint Marie-Béatrice would go and check on the good-for-nothing guards at the sentry posts who were still dozing and by the time she was ready to take off her cornet and put the AK-47 beside her bed and lie down for her well-deserved rest, it was already four o'clock in the morning and the fucking sun was about to pop up again over this cursed country of tribal war, Liberia.

The fact that Marie-Béatrice's convent school managed to withstand the looters for four months was extraordinary. It was a miracle. Feeding fifty people for four months in looted, deserted Monrovia was extraordinary. It was a miracle. Everything Marie-Béatrice had managed to do in the four months under siege was extraordinary. It was a miracle. Marie-Béatrice had performed miraculous feats. She was a saint: Saint Marie-Béatrice.

In spite of what everyone says about Allah never leaving empty a mouth he has created, everyone was speechless and everyone said Marie-Béatrice was a genuine saint for having fed so many people for four months. We don't need to get into an argument, we'll just call her what everyone else called her: Saint Marie-Béatrice. A genuine saint. A saint with a cornet and an AK-47! *Gnamokodé!*

At the beginning of civil war in tribal war Liberia, there were only two factions, Taylor's and Samuel Doe's. The two factions hated each other to death and fought on every front. Prince

Johnson's faction didn't exist back then. Back then, Prince Johnson was part of Taylor's group; he was the most efficient, the most veteran, the most influential general that Taylor had. Right up until the day when the Prince had a revelation. The revelation that he had a mission. A mission to save Liberia. To save Liberia by demanding that power could not be wielded by any warlord who, gun in hand, had fought to liberate Liberia.

That was the day he broke with Taylor, on account of Taylor wanted to be president. Prince Johnson deserted, taking Taylor's best officers and declared himself Taylor's sworn enemy, his bitter opponent. Samuel Doe, the dictator, heard his tirades against Taylor. (A 'tirade' is a long, angry speech, usually of a censorious nature.) And Samuel Doe believed the speeches and thought that in Prince Johnson he had found a natural ally, a friend with whom he could negotiate. Everyone knows what happened, what it cost him. Some officer made a tasty kebab out of Samuel Doe's heart and the royal vulture made a tasty lunch of his eyes one afternoon under the perpetually hazy skies of Monrovia.

After the rift with Taylor, Prince Johnson had to find subsistence for everyone who had followed him, everyone who had put their trust in him, and there was a whole battalion of them. Every man with his people and his family. And, even though Allah never leaves empty a mouth he has created, things were tough. Really tough! *Faforo!*

He started out by attacking one of the NPFL frontier posts so that he could get some duties and taxes for himself, some of the customs duties of independent Liberia. Prince Johnson used maximum force; he sent in several waves of fighters, grenade attacks, mortars, shells. The attack lasted so many days that there was even time to alert the ECOMOG peace-keeping forces, there was even time for them to get there. They arrived with even more maximum forces. The peace-keeping forces didn't keep the peace, they didn't take any unnecessary risks. (I'll explain the word 'risk' for Black Nigger African Natives: it means 'the possibility of suffering harm or loss'.) They weren't bothered about details, they just fired at random, they fired shells at the people doing the attacking and at the people being attacked. They bombed right into the crowd, into the chaos. In a single day they produced loads of innocent victims, more victims than a whole week of the rival factions just fighting with each other. When the uproar died down, the peacekeeping force picked up the wounded. The wounded were evacuated to field hospitals run by ECOMOG. They drew up a report about the area. That was their role, their mission. They ascertained that it was Johnson's territory. He had the upper hand. Therefore Johnson got to take advantage of the customs post. Under their surveillance.

Now that was sorted, Prince Johnson could take care of the dead. We dug a mass grave for our dead, and there were lots of dead. Among the dead were three child-soldiers. Three of the Good Lord's children, according to the saint. They weren't friends of mine. Their names were Mamadou the Mad, John the Proud and Boukary the Damned. They died because that's how Allah wanted things. And Allah is not obliged to be fair about everything he does. And I'm not obliged to say a funeral oration for these three child-soldiers.

The funeral prayers were led by Prince Johnson in person. After the prayers, we stood round the mass grave and raised our guns and fired the parting salvo. ('Salvo', according to the *Petit Robert*, means 'a simultaneous discharge of firearms'.)

But news of the battle for the customs post had got about pretty much everywhere. There'd been so many dead, so much blood and chaos that all the foreign companies started avoiding the customs post.

We (we meaning the members of Johnson's faction) thought it was temporary. For long weeks we waited but nobody showed up at the customs post. There was nothing to loot, so we didn't get paid and we didn't have much to eat. People started complaining. Then the soldiers started deserting. Johnson knew what he was up against, he abandoned the border post. He abandoned the post and all the graves of all those who died in order to capture it. *Faforo!*

There was still the problem of secure and steady profits, and it had to be solved. Even grigrimen like Yacouba were starting to complain; they hadn't got enough to eat and they weren't being paid for the grigris they made. This time, Johnson attacked a gold- and diamond-mining town controlled by ULIMO, who were supporters of Samuel Doe. In his usual way – a dog never gives up his shameless habits – Prince Johnson used maximum force. Grenades and mortars and wave after wave of soldiers. The attackers resisted heroically. There was lots of blood and lots of people dead. The battle lasted several days. The attack lasted so many days that there was even time to alert the ECOMOG peacekeeping forces, there was even time for them to get there. The peacekeeping forces didn't keep the peace, they didn't take any unnecessary risks. They weren't bothered about details, they just fired shells at random, they fired shells at the people doing the attacking and at the people being attacked. They bombed every part of the town, the natives' quarter, full of Black Nigger African Natives, and the miners' quarter. When everything was demolished, when no one was moving any more, not the attackers or the attacked, the peacekeeping forces stopped massacring. They picked up the wounded. The wounded were evacuated to their field hospitals. They drew up a report about the status of forces on the ground. That was their role, their mission, their duty. They ascertained that it was Johnson's territory. Therefore Johnson was awarded control of the town and took over running the mines.

The dead were taken away. Lots of dead. In spite of all the Christian grigris and all the Muslim grigris, four child-soldiers had been blown to bits. They were more than dead, twice as dead. Their remains were dumped in a mass grave with the rest of the dead. As the grave was being filled in, Prince Johnson cried. It was strange seeing a warlord, a warlord like Johnson, crying his heart out because he was so, so angry at ECOMOG. He was wearing his monk's habit for the occasion, and he prayed and made speeches. Like Saint Marie-Béatrice, he said that the child-soldiers were the Good Lord's children. God had given them, God had taken them away. God doesn't always have to be fair. Thanks be to God. It was as good as a funeral oration and that means I don't have to give a funeral oration that I don't want to give. Thanks be to God.

But capturing the gold- and diamond-mining town had caused so much blood, caused so much death, that everyone in the area had run off. Nobody wanted to come back; the bossman partners didn't want to come back. No bossman partners, no mining; no mining, no taxes; no taxes, no American dollars. Johnson found himself back at square one where he was before he seized the town. And time was getting on, and the soldiers and their families and all the child-soldiers and the men in the battalion were starting to grumble. They had made too many worthless sacrifices; they were impatient. Prince Johnson had to do something, he had to find something *gnona-gnona*.

Johnson went back to Monrovia. Everything in Monrovia had been looted, destroyed; the only thing left, the only building left standing, was Saint Marie-Béatrice's convent. Saint Marie-Béatrice was proud; she was provocative, she incited people and defied them.

And there were rumours . . . there were thousands of rumours about all the stuff inside the convent. Masses of food, loads of gold and fat wads of American dollars. All stuffed in huge catacombs that spread out and out and went on and on.

Prince Johnson wanted to find out for himself if the rumours people were spreading were true. He decided to seize the convent. He started by sending an ultimatum to the mother superior, Saint Marie-Béatrice. (An 'ultimatum' is a proposal that is not open to discussion.) This ultimatum demanded that the mother superior officially declare her allegiance to the only legitimate faction in Liberia, meaning Johnson's faction. The mother superior responded that the only thing in the convent was children, women, nuns and a few pitiful wretches. (A 'wretch' is a poor, miserable, unfortunate or unhappy person.) All she asked of any Liberian worthy of the name was a little alms, a little mercy. She didn't have to take sides.

This wasn't an answer, it was a rejection. It was bullshit, it was an affront, an insult. Prince Johnson got angry and, in retaliation, he ruled that the convent school had to pay taxes in the amount of three hundred American dollars to his government as a contribution to the war effort. Immediately.

It wasn't fair; it was 'might is right', just like in the La Fontaine fable 'The Wolf and the Lamb' we learned at school. Now it was the saint's turn to get angry. She screamed, threw her cornet on the ground, and sent the messengers packing ('send packing' means 'dismiss someone abruptly').

'You can tell Johnson that I don't have three hundred dollars. And tell him to leave me alone, leave me in peace to find food for the children, the women and the old. That's all I ask.'

This was the answer Prince Johnson had been hoping for. He decided to attack.

I, Birahima, street kid turned child-soldier, was part of the first unit that led the attack on Saint Marie-Béatrice's convent. There were about ten of us child-soldiers. We were fucked up on drugs, but not too much, because we had to move quietly without attracting the attention of the peacekeeping forces. If we'd been too fucked up, we would have made too much noise and we would have made mistakes. We were strong because we had faith in our grigris. We launched an attack on the convent at three in the morning by moonlight. But there was no element of surprise; the saint had been in the know. We were met by strong resistance. Three of our fighters were massacred and the rest of us had to hit the dirt and retreat on account of the machine-gun fire coming from the convent was very, very heavy. It was the mother superior herself, the saint herself, up there with the machine-gun.

Johnson had his dead picked up *doni-doni* ('*doni-doni*' means 'easy does it') and retreated. He had been tricked, he thought the attack would be a piece of cake for the child-soldiers. But no. He had to be better prepared, mount another attack with more maximum forces and especially more logic and intelligence.

Three child-soldiers had been massacred in spite of the Muslim grigris and the Christian grigris. *Walahé!* We buried them at dawn, in secret. Prince Johnson wore his soutane and he cried and he prayed. The saint said the child-soldiers were God's children. Three of the Good Lord's children had died. I should say their funeral oration, that's the rules. I hadn't been bunking with them very long so I don't really know them well. From what I do know, they were more like the devil's children than the Good Lord's. All three of them were bastards, druggies, criminals, liars. They were cursed. I don't want to say a funeral oration for the damned. And I'm not obliged to. So I'm not going to. *Gnamokodé!*

* * *

For two afternoons Prince Johnson pondered the situation. (To 'ponder' is to reflect or consider with thoroughness and care.) Every afternoon he pondered Saint Marie-Béatrice's convent, pondered Saint Marie-Béatrice kneeling on the stones, her knees black and blue from the stones. And that's when he came up with the solution.

On the third evening, Prince Johnson went back on the attack, still in secret so as not to attract the attention of the ECOMOG peacekeeping forces. Instead of attacking from the front, about twenty soldiers attacked the convent from behind. And by surprise. But no. There was no element of surprise. There she was again, the mother superior in person, the saint, brandishing an AK-47. She machine-gunned hard and long and relentlessly and inflicted heavy losses on the attackers. The second assault, like the first, ended in failure. There was a third night-time secret assault which, like the second, was a fiasco. ('Fiasco', according to my Larousse, means 'a complete failure'.)

Well, then the Prince got really mad, he girded himself. (To 'gird yourself' is a Black Nigger African expression. According to the Glossary, it means to take something seriously, to take the bull by the horns.) In the middle of the day, at noon precisely, he brought out the big guns. The cannons fired and blew the bell tower off the church and destroyed the three-storey building in the middle of the convent. Well, at that point, the saint had to surrender. She came out of the smouldering convent waving a white flag. She was followed by two lines of nuns with cornets, rosaries, the whole works, and they were followed by a horde of miserable wretches.

*   *   *

The ECOMOG forces were surprised by this brutal unforeseen attack. They thought it was a battle royal between the rival factions (a 'battle royal' means 'an intense altercation, a fight to the finish'). ECOMOG sounded the alarm, confined all troops to barracks, and held a meeting of all their top generals that lasted a whole afternoon. When the meeting was over, to their surprise, Monrovia the terrible was dead calm. ECOMOG dispatched a heavily armed patrol to go and see what was happening. The patrol arrived and found Prince Johnson and Saint Marie-Béatrice holding hands and chatting away like old friends who had done their initiation together.

Prince Johnson allowed the saint and her followers to advance until they were within ten metres of him and then he noticed – what a shock! – that the mother superior looked exactly like him, Johnson, just like another him. He had them halt and studied her from head to foot for a long time. There was nothing he could say: they were identical as two drops of water. He had one of his men rip her cornet off and the resemblance was even more disturbing. They were both plump, they had the same nose, the same forehead, the same shape of the skull. For a minute Prince Johnson stood makou, flabbergasted. (I'll explain makou again: it means 'struck with admiration, astonishment, stupor', according to my Glossary.)

Johnson thought for a minute and then threw his arms round the saint's neck and kissed her on the mouth. After lots of warm embraces and kisses, Johnson and the saint held hands and chatted as though they'd known each other for ages and ages.

It was at that moment that the ECOMOG patrol showed up armed to the teeth.

Johnson and the saint were gossiping as though they'd always lived together. Right in front of everyone, the wretches, the nuns in their cornets, the armed guerrillas. Everyone was totally, completely stunned.

General Prince Johnson explained that for a long, long time he had been searching for a woman to command his women's brigade. He offered the saint the position, offered to make her a colonel, offered to pin her stripes on her without further ado, there and then. She refused the rank of colonel. Refused outright; it was not her vocation. She was a saint and she preferred to remain a saint. She preferred to look after the poor, the old, destitute mothers, the nuns and all the pitiful wretches that tribal wars had thrown out into the street. Johnson could not refuse the saint anything; he understood the saint, Saint Marie-Béatrice.

Hand in hand, the two headed back to the convent and wandered around, taking in the massive damage caused by the shelling. Johnson made his apology, expressed his sincere regrets. He was terribly moved; he prayed, he almost cried. After they had walked round the convent three times, Johnson still hadn't noticed a door to the catacombs. Nothing. He came right out and asked. Now that the saint had acknowledged his power, now that the saint was his friend, good governance ('good governance' means 'management') required that all the convent's money be turned over to Johnson's faction. Good governance required that all riches should be controlled by the government.

'What riches?'

'The gold, the fat wads of American dollars, the food that you have stashed in the convent cellars. Where is the door to the catacombs?'

'There are no catacombs.'

'What?'

The mother superior repeated that the convent had no catacombs. There wasn't a word of truth in all the fibs circulating about the convent, she told him. The convent had nothing to hide. Nothing. She invited Johnson to make sure. Johnson had his men turn the convent inside out, the men searched from top to bottom. They didn't find a dollar. Not a single dollar.

Still sceptical ('sceptical' means 'inclined to doubt things that haven't been proved with evidence'), Johnson asked, 'Where did you get the dollars you used to go to market every day?'

'The charity of good people, the alms of the faithful. God never leaves empty a mouth he has created.'

'Well, well.' Johnson turned round and round several times. 'I can't believe it, it can't be true.'

Johnson was sceptical still, sceptical in spite of everything. *Faforo! Gnamokodé!*

Seizing control of the convent had not solved the problem of a steady and secure income for Johnson's faction. On the contrary, now there were hundreds more mouths to feed and not a penny more in the coffers. The NGOs and the good souls who gave money when the mother superior was independent were reluctant to help a convent associated with

Johnson. The pitiful wretches, the destitute mothers and all the children were constantly complaining they were starving. Johnson owed a debt of honour to the convent, the sainted mother superior and all her needy. Johnson would have been only too happy to give the saint her independence, her freedom. But it was too late. The whole country had witnessed the saint's heroic struggle and her subjugation. (According to *Larousse*, 'subjugation' means 'made subservient to, dependent on another person'.) Because of the subjugation, Prince Johnson was obliged to support the saint.

Something had to be done *gnona-gnona* (at the double) for Johnson's faction: a solution had to be found.

The American Rubber Company had the largest plantation in Africa, covering nearly a hundred square kilometres. In fact, the company owned the whole south-east of the country and paid masses of royalties. ('Royalties' is a share in the proceeds paid to an inventor or a proprietor for the right to use his patent or his land.) The royalties were shared between the two old factions, Taylor's and Samuel Doe's. When he had finished breaking with Taylor, Johnson immediately demanded that the royalties be split in three. He convinced the owners to give his faction a share too. The company managers were not prepared to accept this. They hesitated, they feared reprisals from the other two factions. (According to the *Petit Robert*, 'reprisals' means 'retaliation for an injury with the intent of inflicting at least as much injury in return'.) They prevaricated and prevaricated, they beat around the bush in order to delay a decision. So Johnson decided to act like a boy, a boy with a *bangala* that gets hard-ons. (According to the *Glossary*, 'to act like a boy' means 'to be brave'.)

He kidnapped two of the plantation's *toubab* foremen. When he had them safely hidden, he sent an ultimatum to the directors of the plantation. What threats did he make in the ultimatum? He threatened that if he did not get a share of the royalties in twenty-four hours, he would send two men with the two heads of the white bosses on two stakes. Without fail! Without fail! And everyone knew that Johnson the seer was capable of anything; they knew he would do it.

Walahé! The same evening, three *toubab* foremen from the plantation showed up at Johnson's gate. They came as friends, but they didn't come empty-handed. They had briefcases with them, six of them, two briefcases each. We didn't get to see what was in the briefcases . . .

They were in a hurry, they had to see Johnson *gnona-gnona*. Like people with diarrhoea heading for the cesspit behind the huts. Johnson gave them a fine welcome. He chatted to them like close friends. They drank beer together as friends. Johnson slapped them on the back and laughed his big laugh. Then five *toubabs* left the camp, three plus two. Five heads on ten shoulders. *Faforo!*

The royalties arrived bang on time at the end of that month and every month. Johnson decided this was something to be celebrated. He organised a big party in the camp. He paid back wages. Even the child-soldiers got dollars to buy hashish. Everyone was dancing and drinking and eating and getting fucked up on drugs. Then right in the middle of the party,

Prince Johnson brought the festivities to a halt on account of how we had to remember the dead, the countless dead we had left at the border post and in the diamond-mining town. The saint had been invited because now she was a colonel. She refused because she didn't have time because she was always busy taking care of her charges. She would rather Prince Johnson give her the dollars he would have spent on her, because she could put those dollars to a better use. Prince Johnson sent her dollars – genuine American dollars, not Liberian ones.

Everything was cool now. The money wasn't enough, but at least it was regular and everyone got to eat once a day.

But there were lots of small-time thieves and bandits who wanted recognition, they wanted to be factions too. Factions with a right to a share of the royalties, and to get them they started fucking around, breaking into the plantation, kidnapping foremen and demanding ransoms. The ransoms were paid by the plantation bosses in brand-new American dollars.

The reprehensible behaviour of the small-time warlords gave Johnson an idea. Johnson could put a stop to the small-time bandits and get paid protection money. Getting a third of the royalties was good, but protecting the whole plantation against the small-time bandits would be a gold mine. He pondered the idea during his long afternoon sessions of penance.

One morning, Johnson in person, flanked by five four-by-fours, two in front, three behind, all jam-packed with guerrillas armed to the teeth, presented himself at the front gate of the plantation. He wanted to meet with the president.

He was escorted to the president. He talked to the president as a friend. He talked about the activities of the gangs of small-time bandits. He condemned their behaviour, which he said was damaging the good name of the whole of Liberia. These offences had to cease, and he, Johnson, could put a stop to them. He offered his services to put a stop to the activities of the small-time bandits.

Patiently, the president explained to Johnson that handing over the protection of the plantation to him, Johnson, amounted to taking sides, amounted to acknowledging that Johnson was the sole authority in Liberia. That was something he could not do. The other factions wouldn't stand for it.

Johnson replied that the protection would be a secret; that the deal would be a secret. No one would know that Johnson's faction was protecting the plantation. The president explained that he did not have the authority to sign a secret deal with any faction and that anyway everyone would find out about the secret eventually.

Johnson didn't look convinced. Not a bit. He headed back to the camp to think. For three days, during the midday sessions of prayers and penitence, he pondered (remember that every day at noon he knelt on stones to pray and his knees were black and blue from the stones). He tried to think of another way of getting a secret deal to protect the plantation from the small-time crooks. He had to get this secret deal *djogo-djogo* (at all costs). During the three days of prayer, the *djogo-djogo* leitmotif was heard as often as Jesus Christ our Lord. (A 'leitmotif' means 'a dominant and recurring theme, a word or phrase constantly repeated'.) At the end of the third day, his face lit up with a smile. He had thought of a solution.

Two weeks later, the bossmen at the plantation noticed that three labourers had disappeared. They searched for them everywhere without success. Then, one morning, Prince Johnson was seen arriving at the plantation in person and with him were the three poor labourers. The three labourers were in their underpants. Later when he was laughing and drinking beer with the president, Prince Johnson explained that in the course of a routine patrol his men had snatched the workers from a gang of small-time bandits. With great pomp, Johnson handed over the labourers to the president of the plantation. The president thanked Johnson warmly and tried to give him loads of dollars. Johnson refused the dollars. The president couldn't figure it out.

One month later, three white labourers and two black African foremen disappeared from the plantation. The bossmen searched everywhere for them without success. Then, one morning, Prince Johnson arrived at the plantation in person with the five men travelling behind in one of the four-by-fours in his entourage. This time they were completely naked. Johnson explained that his men had managed to rescue them from being tortured by small-time bandits in the nick of time, saved them right at the last minute. Compassionately, Johnson handed them over to the president. Compassionately, because they were not in one piece: the three white labourers had lost their right hands, and the black African foremen had their ears cut off. Twice the president thanked Johnson, thanked him for his compassion and thanked him for having rescued his managers and his labourers from the bandits. This time he definitely wanted to give Johnson a reward. He insisted. But Prince Johnson rejected the brand-new American dollars. He was taking the long view, hoping for more. Still the president couldn't figure it out.

One month and two weeks later, four labourers, three black African foremen and a white *toubab* American disappeared from the plantation. A genuine white man. People searched far and wide in the forests of Liberia without success. Then, one morning, Johnson arrived at the plantation in person. In his convoy, in a four-by-four, were two African foremen. They were naked but they weren't in one piece: their hands and their ears were missing; their hands and their ears had been amputated. There was also one labourer but he wasn't in one piece: his entire body had been amputated. All that was left was the labourer's head on the end of a stake; his entire body was missing. The president roared loudly, roared in terror, indignation, horror. With a smile Johnson calmly explained that it wasn't over, that the bandits were still holding four black Africans and one white man. If his men did not intervene, did not redouble their efforts, it would be too late. Well, at that point, the president got the message loud and clear, he understood totally.

The president grabbed Johnson's hand and led him into an office. They negotiated long and hard and in the end they signed a secret deal. By the terms of the deal, Johnson's faction would protect the plantation against small-time bandits in return for lots of dollars. That same night Johnson showed up at the plantation accompanied by the five other missing employees. There were five people, five naked people, but in one piece. There were no missing ears or hands or entire bodies. Johnson's men had redoubled their efforts. And *djogo-djogo* Johnson had got his secret deal.

At the camp, there was a celebration. Everyone danced. Johnson in his priest's soutane and his kalash danced five times and ended up doing somersaults, doing the monkey dance. *Walahé! Faforo!*

As a secret, the secret remained a secret for five days; by day six, the whole of Liberia from Monrovia to the back end of the country knew Johnson had signed a secret deal with the president of the plantation.

The other factions didn't stand for it. Not at all. Straight away, the leaders of all the factions showed up at the plantation to meet with the president. They handed him their ultimatums written out and in due form. ('In due form' means 'written according to the laws and with all the appended formalities'.) To resolve the situation, the president decided to divide the security guards into three or four units, each one under the control of a different faction. The problem then was how to demarcate (to set the boundaries) between these sections. When he couldn't get the factions to agree to any of his realistic proposals, the president ordered the factions to sort it out among themselves. It was like throwing one bone to three or four vicious guard dogs who were already pawing the ground in anticipation. All over the plantation it was all-out war.

The ECOMOG peacekeeping forces arrived. They bombarded everyone with bombs and everyone ran away. We (we meaning Yacouba, the Muslim grigriman, the crippled crook, and me, the fearless, blameless street kid, the child-soldier) found ourselves in some shitty village on the borders of the plantation on account of our fitting sacrifices had been rejected (meaning by chance). Because Allah doesn't have to be fair in all the things he does.

In this bullshit village – surprise! – we found our friend Sekou. Yacouba's friend Sekou who was a money multiplier like Yacouba. Sekou gave us news of my aunt. She had set off, foot to the road, to walk to Sierra Leone, to my uncle's place in Sierra Leone. So we decided that, since we couldn't go back to Johnson, we had to get to Sierra Leone, *djogo-djogo*, somehow or other.

5

Sierra Leone is a fucked-up mess, a big-time fucked-up mess. A country is a fucked-up mess when you get warlords dividing it up between them like in Liberia, but when you've got political parties and democrats on top of the warlords it's a big-time fucked-up mess. In Sierra Leone, the Kamajors (the hunters' militia) and Kabbah (the democrat) were embroiled in everything, along with warlords like Foday Sankoh, Johnny Koroma and some small-time bandits. That's why people say Sierra Leone isn't a mess, it's a big-time fucked-up mess. In pidgin, the Kamajor are called 'the respectable association of professional traditional hunters'. *Faforo!*

In the name of Allah, the compassionate, the merciful, Let's start at the start.

Sierra Leone is a small fucked-up African state between Guinea and Liberia. For a century and a half, from the start of the English colonisation in 1808 right up to independence on 27 April 1961, the country was a haven of peace, stability and security. Everything was simple back then. From an administrative point of view, there were two only types of people: first, British subjects including colonial English *toubab* colonists and the *creos*, or creoles; and, second, there was the 'protected subjects', Black Nigger Native savages out in the bush. The creoles were descended from freed slaves who came over from America. *Walahé!* The Black Nigger Natives worked as hard as wild beasts. The creoles got all the jobs as civil servants in the government and managers of the commercial businesses. And the colonial English colonists and the thieving double-crossing Lebanese pocketed all the money. The Lebanese didn't show up until much later, between the two big wars. The creoles were rich intelligent Black Niggers who were a lot better than the Black Nigger Native Savages. A lot of them had law degrees and different kinds of diplomas like doctors.

When independence came on 27 April 1961, the Black Nigger Native savages got the right to vote and ever since then Sierra Leone is nothing but *coup d'états* and assassinations and lynchings and executions and all sorts of trouble, a big-time fucked-up mess on account of Sierra Leone is rich in diamonds and gold and all sorts of corruption. *Faforo!*

As soon as the Black Nigger Native savages got independence and the right to vote, they elected the only Black Nigger African Native with a university degree, the only one with a law degree. His name was Milton Margai and he married a white Englishwoman to prove to everyone that he'd completely broken with Black Nigger Native savage habits and traditions.

Milton Margai was already old and a bit wise when they elected him. During his reign as Her Majesty's prime minister, there was some tribal wars but the corruption was manageable. The Mendes, who were people from the same tribe as the prime minister, got favouritism. That was normal. You follow the elephant through the jungle so as not to get wet from the dew (that's a Black Nigger African Native saying that means, when you're close to someone important, you're protected).

When Milton Margai died on 24 April 1964, he was succeeded by his brother Albert Margai known as 'Big Albert'. With Big Albert, the tribal wars and the corruption got worse, got so bad that on 26 March 1967 there was a *coup d'état* and Albert was replaced by Brigadier Juxton-Smith, who was not from the Mende tribe.

Under Brigadier Juxton-Smith corruption was still rife and something had to be done. On 19 April 1968, Brigadier Juxton-Smith was overthrown by a coup organised by the NCOs who founded the Anti-Corruption Revolutionary Movement – the ACRM. Anti-corruption! (*Walahé!* just for that.) But the corruption didn't stop.

On 26 April 1968, Siaka Stevens, who was a Limba, takes over and tries to put a stop to the corruption but he can't do it. In May 1971 another *coup d'état* drives Siaka Stevens out of the palace, out of the capital, but he is brought back safely by Guinean paratroopers. With the protection of the Guinean paras, Siaka Stevens is safe.

He sets up a dictatorship with a one-party system and lots of corruption. Siaka hangs, executes and tortures his opponents. In spite of the corruption, he manages to establish the impression of stability. Siaka Stevens is old, really old, and he makes the most of it to hand over the reins. He has himself replaced as the head of the one-party state by his general and chief of staff, Major General Joseph Saidu Momoh. The general lost the protection of the Guinean government. In August 1985, the general himself admitted that he 'did not have the means to eliminate diamond trafficking'. He meant he couldn't get rid of the corruption.

While all this corruption was going on and all these *coup d'états* were happening one after another, on the sly, people were plotting a bite-that-has-no-teeth (among Black Africans a nasty surprise is known as 'that which bites but has no teeth') against the corrupt scheming regime of Sierra Leone. *Walahé!* Completely on the sly, completely in secret. Foday Sankoh, Corporal Foday Sankoh was about to bite Sierra Leone using no teeth. Corporal Foday Sankoh introduced a third partner to Sierra Leone's dance. Up till then, everything had been simple, very simple: there were only two dancers, only two underhand partners, the government and the army. If the dictator in power got too corrupt and too rich, there was a *coup d'état* and he was replaced by a general. If he hadn't already been assassinated, the dictator took the money and fled without further ado. When the guy who replaced him got too corrupt, too rich, there was another different coup and someone else replaced him and, if he hadn't already been assassinated, he did a runner with the *liriki*, the cash.

160

And so on. Foday Sankoh fucked up this private dance when he introduced another whore to the dance: the people, the poor people, the Black Nigger Native savage Sierra Leonean bushmen.

First off, who is Foday Sankoh, Corporal Foday Sankoh? *Gnamokodé!*

Foday Sankoh, a Temne, joins the army of Sierra Leone in 1956. In 1962 he gets his corporal's stripes (in his long and extraordinary career he never gets any more stripes), and in 1963 he is sent with a contingent of soldiers from Sierra Leone on a peacekeeping mission to Congo. The absolutely outrageous way that Patrice Lumumba (Congo's first prime minister) is assassinated sickens him, but makes him think. He comes to the conclusion that the vast machinery of the UN always serves the interests of European colonial *toubab* colonists and never the interests of the poor Black Nigger Native savages.

When he gets back to Sierra Leone, he becomes aware of the suffering of his people and the appalling corruption that rules his country. That's when he decides to go into politics.

In 1965, Foday Sankoh is suspected of being involved in the military coup against Margai led by Colonel John Bangoura. Sankoh is arrested and released. In 1971, he is involved in the *coup d'état* mounted by Momoh against Siaka Stevens. He is arrested and banged up for six long years. While he's in prison, he reads Mao Tse-Tung and other theorists of the popular revolution and he thinks. He thinks and thinks and he comes to a conclusion. A military coup that changes the people at the top won't put an end to Sierra Leone's corrupt bastard regime. It will take more than that, it will take a popular revolution. Foday Sankoh dedicates himself to the popular revolution.

Starting in the east of the country, Foday Sankoh eventually settles in Bô, the second biggest city in Sierra Leone. Working undercover as a photographer, he circulates his ideas until 1990. At the beginning of 1991, he recruits an army of three hundred people, men he calls the freedom fighters of the Revolutionary United Front (the pidgin abbreviation is RUF). He trains his men to be genuine proper soldiers. The freedom fighters get their hands on modern weapons by staging a string of ambushes, the modern weapons replace their machetes. On 23 March 1991 Foday Sankoh starts a civil war on the Liberian border, supported by the Liberian warlord Taylor.

The astonished president, Joseph Momoh, panics, protests Taylor's involvement, and demands the support of the other members of CDEAO. Then he sends thousands of soldiers to the border to hold off the RUF rebels, to repel the 'invaders', but all the soldiers desert and join the RUF freedom fighters. There is nothing Joseph Momoh can do. Sierra Leone is on the brink of collapse. Joseph Momoh is ousted from power by a coup. He takes off *gnona-gnona* with the loot and is replaced by Captain Valentine Strasser.

Captain Strasser has two policies. Number one: deal with the bane of corruption ('bane' means 'a constant annoyance or danger'). Number two: deal with Foday Sankoh and the RUF. To fight Foday Sankoh, Strasser recruits fourteen thousand kids. These starving kids are *sobels* – soldiers by day and rebels (looting and thieving) by night. But they all desert and join the RUF freedom fighters, and on the morning of 15 April 1995 Foday Sankoh launches an offensive, heading west in the direction of the capital, Freetown. Foday Sankoh and his RUF, without firing a shot, take the strategic town of Mile-Thirty-Eight and the surrounding gold-rich, diamond-rich region with all the coffee plantations and the cocoa plantations and the palm oil plantations. From that day on, he doesn't give a shit what happens next on account of he controls the useful part of Sierra Leone.

Walahé! Valentine Strasser hasn't got a penny to his name, nothing, not a red cent. He's annoyed, really fucked off, and he decides to play the democracy game. He gives the go-ahead to multi-party politics, holds a National Conference (National Conferences were the big political meetings that every African country held in 1994 where everybody just said the first thing that came into their heads). With the support of the UN, Valentine Strasser decides to hold free and fair elections. Foday Sankoh isn't duped by the democracy game. No sir. He doesn't want anything to do with any of it. He doesn't want a National Conference, he doesn't want free and fair elections. He doesn't want anything. He controls the part of the country with the diamonds; he controls the useful part of Sierra Leone. He doesn't give a fuck. What he wants first of all is for the UN representative from the Congo, his bête noire, to be expelled from the country ('bête noire' is the person you hate most). Foday Sankoh has got no intention of giving up the gold and diamond mines for as long as the UN representative is stationed in Sierra Leone.

Valentine Strasser is in trouble, he doesn't know what to do, but the most important thing is to protect the capital and the little bit of land he still controls. First he appeals to Gurkhas from Nepal, then the South African mercenaries, the 'executive outcomes' of South African society, the Boers. He never gets to look any further on account of he is ousted by his aide Julius Mananda Bio, vice-president of the National Provisional Ruling Council. Captain Strasser hightails it out of there *gnona-gnona* with the loot, like a thief.

The date is 16 January 1996 and there's Mananda Bio in the palace, Lumley Beach Palace (that's the name of the residence where the president, the leader of Sierra Leone, lives). The UN and the CDEAO put pressure on Mananda Bio, forcing him to stick to the plans Strasser had made to hold free and fair elections on February 26. On January 28, Mananda Bio starts negotiations with a delegation sent by Foday Sankoh. Foday Sankoh doesn't want free and fair elections. He doesn't want them, no sir. (He doesn't give a fuck, he controls the useful part of Sierra Leone.)

In spite of his protests, the first round of the presidential election goes ahead while negotiations between Mananda Bio and Foday Sankoh are still going on. Sankoh fulminates (to 'fulminate' is to explode in a thunderous rage and start threatening and insulting). Before negotiations are over, he has to stop the free and fair elections, he has to stop the second round. How can he stop the democratic elections? How can he stop the second round from going ahead?

He considers the problem, and when Foday Sankoh puts his mind to something he gives up tobacco, alcohol and women. *Walahé!* He goes on the wagon and locks himself away for days and days.

At the end of the fifth day of this draconian routine ('draconian' means 'exceedingly harsh, very severe'), the solution spontaneously comes to his lips in a simple slogan: 'no hands, no elections'. It was obvious: someone with no arms couldn't vote. All Foday Sankoh had to do was cut off the arms of as many people, as many of the citizens of Sierra Leone, as possible. Every Sierra Leone prisoner had his hands cut off before being sent back into the territory occupied by government forces. Foday gave the orders and methods and the orders and the methods were enforced. The 'long sleeve, short sleeve' policy was put into action. 'Short sleeve' was when you cut off the whole forearm; 'long sleeve' was when you cut off both hands at the wrist.

Amputations were rife, and they were carried out with no quarter, no mercy. If a woman showed up with a baby on her back, the woman's hands were amputated and the baby's hands too. It didn't matter how old the baby was on account of how you might as well amputate baby citizens because they'll be voters some day.

Non-governmental organisations suddenly noticed the arrival of large numbers of long- and short-sleeved armless people. They panicked and started putting pressure on Mananda Bio. Mananda Bio panics, Mananda Bio wants to negotiate but he needs someone Foday Sankoh will trust, someone whose moral authority is universally recognised.

He goes knocking on the door of the wise man of Africa in Yamoussoukro.

The wise man's name is Houphouët-Boigny. He is a dictator, a respectable old man, bleached and grizzled first by corruption, later by old age and too much wisdom. Houphouët takes the problem seriously: it's urgent. *Gnona-gnona*, Houphouët sends Amara, his minister for foreign affairs, to fetch Foday Sankoh from his *maquis* deep in the wild, impenetrable forests (a *maquis* is a hard to find place where freedom fighters hang out).

Amara brings Foday Sankoh back in one piece, in the flesh, to the old dictator of Yamoussoukro. The old dictator kisses him on the mouth and welcomes him with wanton extravagance ('wanton' means so astonishingly excessive it seems to go against the ordinary). He affords him every luxury, gives him stacks of money, and entertains him with the sort of style that only an old and true dictator can offer. Foday Sankoh who never set foot in a five-star hotel in his whole life; Foday Sankoh who had it tough, his whole life, is happy, jubilant. Foday has a surfeit (a lot) of everything and gets through a surfeit. He gets through a surfeit of cigarettes, alcohol, mobile phones, and he especially gets through an inordinate surfeit of women. Under these extraordinary conditions, he agrees to a ceasefire.

The second round of the presidential election goes ahead. Despite all the amputations of lots of the citizens of Sierra Leone, the little people are excited about voting. They think the election will put an end to their martyrdom, to their suffering. It was an illusion. Everyone goes to the polling booths. Even the armless people, especially the armless people. The armless people get to vote anyway. They go into the voting booth with a friend or a brother who does the voting for them.

On 17 March 1996, Ahmad Tejan Kabbah is elected with 60% of the vote. The democratically elected president moves into Lumley Beach palace. He immediately sends a delegation to Yamoussoukro to negotiate.

Foday Sankoh refuses to recognise his authority. As far as he is concerned, there were no elections, there is no president. (He doesn't give a fuck, he controls the useful part of Sierra Leone.)

After a month of long negotiations, Foday Sankoh is persuaded to see sense. The details are hammered out in the final communiqué. The communiqué is published. Foday Sankoh agrees to everything and is allowed to go back to his hotel and his wanton luxury, his alcohol, his cigarettes, his women and his mobile phones.

One month later, in a sensational declaration, Foday Sankoh reneges on everything, he fails to keep his word. He says that he never agreed to anything, never accepted the elections, never acknowledged Ahmad Tejan Kabbah. He's going to call off the ceasefire.

Negotiations start again. They are meticulous (precise, rigorous). In the end, they come to an end. The final communiqué is discussed, point by point, comma by comma, for a long, long time. Foday Sankoh enthusiastically agrees to the communiqué. Everyone congratulates Foday Sankoh. Houphouët-Boigny kisses him on the mouth. They send him back to his hotel, to his wanton luxury, his quirks and his vices (doing sex that deviates from morality). One month later – bang! – everyone is back at square one. Foday Sankoh says he never agreed to the elections, never accepted the results of the election, never acknowledged Ahmad Tejan Kabbah as president. Never! (He doesn't give a fuck, he controls the useful part of Sierra Leone!)

All the people who were in the negotiations scurry back to Yamoussoukro. Negotiations begin again. Laboriously, point by point, every aspect of the agreement is thrashed out. They finally, finally, agree on a final communiqué. The talks are more closely fought than ever. This time it's for real, that's why they have to agree on everything, even on the tiniest details. Everyone is happy. The talks were difficult, but they nonetheless reached a definitive result.

Faforo! Two months later, when everyone thought everything had been agreed, the ceasefire, the negotiation process, Foday Sankoh reappears with a thundering declaration. He didn't accept anything, he didn't sign anything, he doesn't acknowledge anything, the elections, the president, anything. His freedom fighters go back to fighting. (He doesn't give a fuck, he controls the useful part of Sierra Leone!)

The negotiators scurry back to the Hotel Ivoire, the palace where Foday Sankoh is staying with all his vices. But there's no sign of Foday! They search all over the place; in the seediest, sleaziest parts of Treichville. (Treichville is the red-light district of Abidjan, the capital of Côte d'Ivoire.) No sign of Foday. They suspect he's been kidnapped. The police are under serious pressure. Everyone fears for his life. Dictator

Houphouët-Boigny is really embarrassed on account of how he was Foday's host so it's his responsibility. He rages against the police. They search and search. Still no Foday!

Three weeks later, as the search is still going on, they get news that Foday Sankoh has been arrested in Lagos, Nigeria, for gunrunning. What the hell was he doing in Nigeria? *Walahé!* The Nigerian dictator, Sani Abacha, is Foday Sankoh's sworn enemy. What the fuck was Foday thinking sticking his head in the alligator's mouth? Into the mouth of the alligator dictator Sani Abacha?

The reason is the petty jealousy of two dictators: dictator Houphouët-Boigny and dictator Sani Abacha. Sani Abacha's troops were the ones fighting in Sierra Leone, but it was Houphouët-Boigny who got to host the negotiations. It was Sani Abacha's countrymen who were dying in Sierra Leone, but it was Houphouët-Boigny that everyone was talking about in the international press; it was Houphouët-Boigny that everyone was calling 'the wise man of Africa'. Like it says in the Black Nigger African Native proverb, Sani Abacha was the one standing out in the rain, but Houphouët-Boigny was the one pulling fish from the river. Or like they say in French, Houphouët-Boigny was the one feathering his nest. To put an end to this situation, the dictator Sani Abacha set up a bona fide trap for Foday Sankoh. He sent a secret agent to Abidjan who secretly offered Foday a deal, a bum deal. He told Foday Sankoh to go to Lagos in secret. He'd be met by Sani Abacha and they could discuss the best way to get ECOMOG troops out of Sierra Leone. Foday Sankoh fell for it. When he arrived in Lagos, he was arrested as a gunrunner.

Locked up – click! – double-locked. With Foday Sankoh under lock and key, out of the way, they started to make contact with his supporters on the ground thinking they would be more malleable (submissive). But Foday's supporters refused to co-operate. They refused to take part in any talks without their leader. And from his cell, Foday made his big drum of a voice heard. His grave, booming voice that says no, nothing but no.

Sani Abacha the dictator, embarrassed, not knowing what to do with the intractable Foday Sankoh (according to the *Petit Robert*, 'intractable' means 'difficult to manage or govern, troublesome'), hands him over to the Sierra Leonean authorities, to the democratically elected president of Sierra Leone Ahmad Tejan Kabbah. Tejan Kabbah puts Foday Sankoh on the wagon. He locks him up good and tight and denies him women, cigarettes, alcohol and visits. Still Foday Sankoh says no, no, nothing but no. He has no intention of agreeing to anything, conceding anything. He calls on the new wise man of Africa, the new elder statesman of African dictators, the dictator Eyadema. Houphouët-Boigny who had held this role for many years having kicked the bucket in the interim ('kick the bucket' means 'die'), leaving to his heirs and successors one of the most colossal fortunes in black Africa, more than three thousand five hundred billion CFA francs!

Right now it's 1994, but let's jump ahead.

The new wise man of Africa, the dictator Eyadema, will summon Foday Sankoh to Lomé, the capital of Togo. He'll set him up again with all the things he likes, all his vices. He'll offer him everything: women, cigarettes, mobile phones and lots of negotiations. He'll be a free man. Talks will start again from square one. Foday Sankoh the warlord will still say no, nothing but no. He won't want to acknowledge the outcome of the elections. He won't want a ceasefire. He won't agree to anything. (He won't give a fuck, he'll still control the useful part of Sierra Leone.)

So the dictator Eyadema will come up with a great idea, a brilliant idea. An idea that will be actively supported by the USA, France, Britain and the UN. The idea is to suggest a change to the changes that doesn't change anything. With the agreement of the international community, Eyadema will offer the warlord Foday Sankoh the post of vice-president of the Republic of Sierra Leone with jurisdiction over all the mines that he already seized by force, with jurisdiction over all the useful parts of Sierra Leone that he already controls. This is a huge change to the changes that amounts to no change at all. No change in his position as a warlord: he won't be charged with anything. No change in the warlord's riches. So long as there is to be a general amnesty, Foday Sankoh will say yes, straight off, yes and yes. With no one twisting his arm or boring him to death with talk, he'll say yes. He'll acknowledge the government. He'll agree to the ceasefire. He'll agree to disarming his freedom fighters. Too bad for the 'short sleeves' and the 'long sleeves', too bad for the pitiful wretches.

That's how it goes, that's the price to pay to have Foday Sankoh march into Freetown wearing both hats, one as vice-president of the unified democratic Republic of Sierra Leone and one as administrator of all the mines in Sierra Leone.

This is the political ruse that will finally put an end to the civil war in Sierra Leone. *Faforo! Gnamokodé!* But we're not there yet.

All that comes after, long, long after. After we'd ventured through the territories of Foday Sankoh and his freedom fighters. We means Yacouba, the crippled crook, the money multiplier, the Muslim grigriman, and me, Birahima, the fearless, blameless street kid, the small-soldier. We were looking for my aunt Mahan who had left Liberia and was trying to get to my uncle in Sierra Leone. *Walahé!*

We started venturing our way round Foday Sankoh territory just two weeks after 15 April 1995. April 15 was the day of Foday Sankoh's lightning strike that delivered the knock-out blow to the Sierra Leone authorities and let him get his hands on the useful part of Sierra Leone. We were captured by RUF freedom fighters in a town called Mile-Thirty-Eight, about thirty-eight miles outside Freetown. Freetown is the capital of the cursed fucked-up country of Sierra Leone.

The big boss of the area and of the men who captured us in Mile-Thirty-Eight was called Tieffi. General Tieffi was the spitting image of Foday Sankoh. Same grey beard, same hunter's Phrygian bonnet, same satisfaction from good living, the same smile and the same hair-raising laugh, a laugh so surprising it's almost scary.

Straight off, he wanted to pack us off to the abattoir; that's the place where they cut off the hands and arms of Sierra Leonean citizens to stop them from voting. Luckily, Yacouba had a feeling. He resigned his identity as a Muslim grigriman with the power to stop bullets and instead handed over his fake identity card that made him a citizen of Côte d'Ivoire. Tieffi was happy to find out we were Ivoirians. He liked Houphouët-Boigny, the president of Côte d'Ivoire. On account of Houphouët was rich and wise and had even built a basilica. He told us we were lucky because if we were Guinean or even foreign, they'd have cut off our hands anyway, because Guinea was sticking its nose into the internal affairs of Sierra Leone. Yacouba tightened his grip on our Guinean identity cards that he'd had the instinct not to hand over.

Yacouba was packed off to the grigrimen's huts where they get to eat well. He got to work. He made an unbeatable grigri for General Tieffi.

Me, the fearless, blameless street kid, I was sent straight off to join the child-soldier unit where they gave you a kalash, the whole works.

I wanted to be one of the young lycaeons of the revolution. That's the child-soldiers who are given the most inhuman jobs. Tough jobs like putting a bee into someone's eye, like it says in the Black Nigger African Native savage proverb. Tieffi had a huge grin.

'You know what it is lycaeon?' he asked.

I told him no.

'Well now, lycaeons are wild dogs that hunt in packs. They gobble everything; mother, father, all and everything. When they finish sharing a victim, every lycaeon goes off to clean his self. If one comes back with blood on his fur, even one drop of blood, they think he is wounded and he's gobbled up by the others right there. That's what it is. Got it? They have no mercy. Your mother alive?'

173

'No.'

'Your father alive?'

I said no again.

Tieffi burst out laughing.

'You got no luck, little Birahima, you can never be a brave young lycaeon of the revolution. Your mother and your father already dead, dead and buried. To be a brave young lycaeon of the revolution, you must first kill with your bare hands (with your own hands, understand?), kill one of your own parents (father or mother), and only afterwards be initiated.'

'I could be initiated like all the young lycaeons.'

He burst out laughing again and he said, 'No and no. You are not Mende, you do not understand Mende, you are Malinké. The ceremonies of initiation are sung and danced in Mende. At the end of the ceremonies, a lump of meat is eaten by the young initiate. The hunk of meat is prepared by sorcerers with many ingredients and perhaps human flesh. Malinkés dislike eating this meat, Mendes do not. In tribal wars, a little human meat is necessary. It makes the heart hard, very hard, and protects against bullets. The best protection against whistling bullets is probably a piece of human meat. For example, I, Tieffi, never go to the front, never go to battle without a calabash (a bowl) of human blood. A calabash of human blood makes you strong, makes you fierce, makes you cruel, and protects you from whistling bullets.'

The initiation of the young lycaeon takes place in the forest. He wears a raffia tunic, he sings, and dances hard and fast, he cuts off the hands and arms of citizens of Sierra Leone. After, he eats a hunk of meat, a hunk of meat that is surely human flesh. For the initiates, this meat serves as the fine and delicious end to the initiation ceremony. *Gnamokodé!*

I couldn't join the elite child-soldiers, the young lycaeons. I wasn't entitled to the double rations of food, loads of drugs, the triple salary of the young lycaeons. I was useless, a nobody.

I was part of the brigade in charge of protecting the mines. The people who worked in the mines were half-slaves. They got paid, but they weren't free to leave.

Let's go back to the government, to the politics of this fucked-up country of damned souls and *cacabas* (madmen).

On 17 March 1996, Ahmad Tejan Kabbah is elected with 60% of the vote. The democratically elected president moves into Lumley Beach Palace on April 15. In the palace he is alone face to face with his destiny, meaning – like all democratically elected presidents – face to face with the army of Sierra Leone. The palace is haunted by the ghosts of all his predecessors who ran away or were gunned down there. He can't sleep; he sleeps the sleep of the caiman, one eye half-open. He thinks a lot about how to end the hostile standoff with the army of Sierra Leone.

Ever since the tenth century, there has been freemasonry in Sierra Leone, like in every other West African country. A freemasonry of hunters, of great initiates and of the most powerful sorcerers and seers, it's called the Kamajor. Ahmad Tejan Kabbah thinks about the Kamajor, the association of skilled traditional hunters. He summons them to the palace. Kabbah talks tough with the hunters. The hunters agree to put themselves at the service of the palace. The hunters trade their homemade rifles for AK-47s. From that day on, Kabbah, the elected president, can sleep with both eyes closed, sleep like a milkmaid's baby. (A milkmaid's baby sleeps in peace because he knows whatever happens he will have milk.) From that day on there were two camps and five players in the country. In the first camp, the democratically elected power, the Sierra Leonean army commanded by the chief of staff Johnny Koroma, ECOMOG (the peacekeeping force who never keep the peace) and the Kamajor or traditional hunters. The second faction was made up of Foday Sankoh's RUF. In other words it was everyone against Foday Sankoh. There really were five players and two factions. But all the players kept coming and going in the vastness of Sierra Leone. All the players were busy bleeding the people of Sierra Leone dry.

We were at Mile-Thirty-Eight. (We means the crippled crook and me, the blameless, fearless street kid.) In the stronghold of the RUF, the stronghold of Foday Sankoh.

One night, just after the moon went down, a lot of whispering and hissing started up in the forest all around the camp right up close. No one took any notice. There was the crack of gunfire from the sentries. No one took any notice. Everyone went right on sleeping the sleep of a Senegalese champion wrestler who's beaten every wrestler of his generation. There was gunfire every night on account of how every night you had thieves sneaking round near the mines. The intermittent gunfire didn't stop the whispering.

By dawn, there were kalashes firing all over the village

and we heard the song of the hunters, taken up by a thousand voices. The camp was being attacked, surrounded by the Kamajors. Their trick was to arrive in the middle of the night and lay siege to a village and then attack at dawn. We were taken by surprise. We knew bullets couldn't kill the hunters. The child-soldiers panicked and ran around crying, 'The bullets can't kill them! The hunters are bullet-proof!' And then people were absconding in all directions in a mad rush. By noon, the Kamajors had cut off all the roads and taken all the battle stations. All our leaders had skedaddled.

The hunters, the Kamajors, organised a feast like they always do whenever they have a victory. They had AK-47s, but that's the only modern thing they had. Their uniforms were tunics with thousands of grigris and claws and animal hair pinned to them and they all wore Phrygian bonnets. They were singing and dancing and firing their guns into the air.

After the feast, they took over running the camp, the huts, the mines. They gathered us, all us prisoners, together. I was a prisoner and so was my protector Yacouba. We were prisoners of the Kamajors.

The offensive mounted by the professional traditional hunters had cost the lives of six child-soldiers. I decided it's my duty to say a funeral oration for one of the six; because he was the one who was my friend. At night, in the huts, he had time to tell me his journey lots of times. ('Journey', according to the *Petit Robert*, means 'a process or course likened to travelling: *the journey of life*.') I'm only saying his funeral oration because I'm not obliged to say a funeral oration for the others. I don't have to, same as Allah doesn't have to always be fair about everything.

Among the dead was the body of Johnny Thunderbolt.

No kidding! No kidding! It was a teacher's *gnoussou-gnoussou* that did for Johnny Thunderbolt, that led him to be a child-soldier. Yes, it was a teacher's vagina that led him to the child-soldiers. This is how.

Johnny Thunderbolt's real name was Jean Bazon. He was called Jean Bazon when he was going to school in Man before joining the child-soldiers. In his third year in primary school, there was a podium in the classroom. The teacher's desk was on the podium. It was hot, really hot and the headmistress let herself go, let the breeze up between her legs, opened her legs. Too wide. And the kids had fun crawling around under the desks having a good look at what was on display. Any excuse was a good excuse. They'd laugh uproariously, loud and full, about it at break time.

One morning in the middle of lessons, Jean dropped his pencil on the ground. Automatically, not for any bad reason (absolutely not), he bent down to pick up his pencil. But that day was not his lucky day, it was the moment the teacher had been waiting for. Someone had told her, or she'd just noticed the prank. She was hysterical, furious. ('Hysteria' is a state of great agitation bordering on madness.) 'Pervert! Bastard! Pervert!' she screamed. And she laid into him with anything she could lay her hands on, the ruler, her hands, her feet. She beat Bazon savagely, like an animal. Jean Bazon ran away. The teacher told a lanky boy named Touré to go after him. A couple of hundred yards on, Jean Bazon stopped, picked up a stone and – wham! – he threw it right in Touré's face. Touré dropped, dropped like a ripe fruit, dropped dead. Jean kept running like mad until he got to his aunt's house. 'I killed someone, I killed one of my friends from school.' The aunt panicked and hid Jean with a neighbour. The police came looking for the young delinquent. 'We haven't seen him since yesterday,' his aunt said.

In the middle of the night, Jean left Man for a nearby village on the road to Guinea. From there he was able to take a truck incognito (without being recognised) heading for his uncle's place in N'Zérékoré in Guinea. It was not a quiet trip on account of the truck was stopped by road-blockers with kalashes at the Liberia/Guinea border. The road-blockers took everything they had, they even took parts of the truck. Then a bunch of guerrillas showed up and the road-blockers made a run for it. The passengers were picked up by the guerrillas and taken to their camp. The guerrillas told the passengers that those who wanted could go back to Man on foot, it was a two-day walk. Bazon thought: 'Me go back to Man? Never, I want to be a child-soldier.' And that's how Jean Bazon joined the child-soldiers, where he became Johnny Thunderbolt.

What Jean Bazon did to earn the nickname Johnny Thunderbolt is another story, it's a long story. I don't feel like telling it and I'm not obliged to. The body of Johnny Thunderbolt was lying there and it made me sad, really sad. I cried my heart out to see Johnny lying there dead like that. All on account of the bullets not being able to kill the hunters and Johnny not knowing that it was the hunters attacking.

Walahé! Walahé! Bismillâh irrahmân ir-rahîm! In the name of Allah, the compassionate, the merciful!

There were women and girls at Mile-Thirty-Eight. The women did the cooking; the girls were child-soldiers like us. The girls had their own unit. The unit was run by a vicious cow who was trigger-happy with a machine-gun. (A 'cow' is a fat woman with bad manners.) Her name was Sister Hadja Gabrielle Aminata.

Sister Hadja Gabrielle Aminata was one-third Muslim, one-third Catholic and one-third animist. She was a colonel on account of she had lots of experience with young girls because over twenty years she'd excised nearly a thousand girls. ('Excise' is the part of the girls' initiation where they amputate the clitoris.)

The girls all lived together in an old girls' boarding school in Mile-Thirty-Eight. It was made up of about ten houses built around a rectangular concession. There was a sentry post at each corner of the cloister defended with sandbags. The sentry posts were manned day and night by girl-soldiers. The camp was surrounded by human skulls on stakes all round the boundary. That's tribal wars for you. It was kind of a boarding school that Sister Aminata ruled with a rod of iron.

Reveille was at four in the morning. All the young girls did their ablutions ('ablutions' means 'washing of the body as part of a religious rite') and bowed for the Muslim prayer even if the girl wasn't a Muslim. Because waking up early made the girls strong and the morning ablutions got rid of the smell of pee that always hangs around Black Nigger

Native girls. After the communal prayer, there was cleaning fatigue, then exercises, then drill. Sister Aminata yelled a lot during drill and thumped any young girl whose manoeuvres were half-hearted. Afterwards, all the girls lined up and marched down to the river at the double singing patriotic Sierra Leonean songs. At the river they all bathed in lots of water. They marched back to the headquarters at the double singing patriotic songs like when they left. After lunch, the girls did normal lessons: reading, sewing and cooking. Sister Aminata, armed with her AK-47, kept an eye on everything.

In her long career as an excisor, Sister Gabrielle Aminata had always refused, downright refused, to excise any girl who had lost her virginity. That's why she got it into her head, during all the troubles and the tribal wars, that she had to defend the virginity of her girls at any price until peace returned to the beloved motherland of Sierra Leone. She defended it with a kalash. This mission to defend her girls' virginity with a kalash was vigorously enforced without a grain of pity. She was like a mother to the girls in the unit, she was jealous and protected the girls in the unit from any advances, even from chiefs like Tieffi. Sister Gabrielle machine-gunned any girl who strayed from the path. And mercilessly machine-gunned anyone who raped any of her girls.

One day, a young girl was found raped and decapitated between three labourers' camps. Eventually they found out the poor girl was called Sita and she was eight years old. Sita had been horribly killed in a way you wouldn't want to see.

Even someone whose whole life is blood like Sister Hadja Gabrielle Aminata cried her heart out when she saw it.

For a week, a whole week, everyone rushed round trying to find out who was guilty of the crime. But in vain, nothing came of the investigations.

At the beginning of the next week, things started to go from bad to worse. Any workers who ventured beyond the camp at night to relieve themselves never came back. He'd be found dead the next morning, emasculated (with no penis) and decapitated like poor Sita with a note on him that read: 'The work of the *dja*, the avenging spirit of Sita.' The workers panicked. Child-soldiers were dispatched to guard them. Every night the child-soldiers were overpowered by masked figures who came and kidnapped workers from the camps. In the morning, the victims were found murdered, emasculated and decapitated like little Sita, and there was always a note explaining that this was the work of Sita's *dja*.

The workers went on strike, some even went and hid out in neighbouring camps. It was no good, it didn't work: wherever they went, death was following behind.

This was in General Tieffi's time. General Tieffi, supreme master of the district and all its inhabitants, investigated the case himself and he eventually figured it out. He called an assembly of all those living in the huts, and Sister Gabrielle Aminata and her closest colleagues were invited. The women all arrived with AK-47s, and the colonel herself came in hajj dress, meaning dressed like a Muslim woman on her way back from Mecca. She carried her kalash under the frills of her skirts. That's tribal wars that does that.

All afternoon there was a heated palaver. At sunset, the camp workers finally convicted some poor wretch. He was guilty of the death of little Sita. He and no one else. He was handed over to Sister Gabrielle Aminata. What she did to the poor wretch doesn't need to be told. I don't have to tell everything in my bullshit story. *Faforo!*

When the Kamajors arrived at Mile-Thirty-Eight, some of them, seeing all these young virgin girls in one place, were drooling with desire, jumping for joy. Here were lots of girls to marry. Right away, Sister Gabrielle Aminata had a meeting with the general, the master hunter in command of the regiment of hunters. She told him she did not have any marriageable girls, only girls she had to keep on the path of righteousness. She intended to safeguard the virginity of all of her girls until peace came. When peace returned, she herself would excise the girls before returning them to their families where they would be ready to make proper, decent marriages. She warned him that she would ruthlessly and summarily execute any hunter who tried to corrupt one of her girls. Her threats had the lecherous hunters in fits of laughter. ('Lecherous' means 'given to excessive indulgence in sexual activity'.)

One day, a girl ventured outside the compound. She was with her mother who had come to visit her. She was hunted down by lecherous hunters who caught her and took her to a cacao plantation. In the cacao plantation they raped her, gang-raped her. Sister Aminata found the girl lying in her own blood. Her name was Mirta, she was twelve years old. Sister Aminata Gabrielle went to see the generalissimo, the master hunter, the leader of all the hunters of Sierra Leone. The generalissimo promised to investigate. The investigation didn't go anywhere. Night and day, there was a hunter always loitering round the girls' barracks. Sister Aminata was very suspicious of him. They lured him into a trap. They sent out a girl and she wandered around the compound. The hunter threatened her with a kalash and took her to the cacao plantation. Just when the lecher was about to jump on her, girls came out of the forest armed to the teeth and arrested him. They tortured the hunter and made him confess. He had been involved, well and truly involved in the gang-rape of Mirta. With a hail of gunfire, Aminata Gabrielle shut him up permanently. They threw his body over the wall of the camp into the next street, shouting indiscriminately (at random), 'He was involved in Mirta's rape.' When the hunters saw their friend's corpse, there was an outcry. The hunters rioted and attacked Sister Gabrielle's compound, they laid siege to it night and day. Three times in one night, Sister Gabrielle herself walked out of the compound and spread panic among the hunters. Every time she came out, she killed at least three men. Enraged, the hunters showed up at the compound with an armoured car. Sister Aminata, in her hajj robes, carrying her kalash, managed to crawl as far as the armoured car. She climbed on to the hood and tried to kill the driver, but a hunter lying in ambush fired and she fell down dead. She died like a soldier.

Sister Aminata Gabrielle's corpse threw the association of Sierra Leonean hunters into terrible confusion. Sister Aminata Gabrielle was a woman, but a woman who died a war hero.

The code of honour of the hunters demands that all those who die as heroes be treated as master hunters and buried with all the honours of a master hunter. But the rules said a woman couldn't be buried as a master hunter. The question was put to the generalissimo of the hunters. His response was unambiguous (categorical, unequivocal). Though she was a woman, she had held out for two weeks against two regiments of hunters; she had killed nine hunters in nocturnal sorties and she had died capturing an armoured car. She richly deserved to be buried as a hero, a master hunter. She deserved it no matter what her sex.

That's why Sister Aminata was given the funeral of a master hunter, of a great master hunter.

From the moment she was considered a master hunter, she was considered to have lots of *gnamas* (the avenging spirits of men and animals that you've killed). These had to be gathered up, and they were gathered up in a small gourd. The *sora*, the hunters' *griot*, came to deliver her funeral oration. The hunters, in order of rank, walked around the body. As the *sora* continued to sing the magical verses, the hunters walked round the body carrying their homemade rifles diagonally across their chests, marking the rhythm of the song by swaying their torsos, once to the left, once to the right.

After the dance, the corpse was immediately carried to the edge of the grave. Three master hunters came and bent over the grave of Sister Aminata. They removed her heart, gathered it up and, taking it, left the ceremony. Far from the ceremony the heart was fried, then placed in oil in a *kanari*. The *kanari* was sealed tight and buried in the earth.

As soon as the three master hunters had left, the hunters bid farewell to Sister Hadja, Gabrielle, Aminata, the excisor, the woman who was buried with the honours of a master hunter. All the hunters bade farewell, firing their homemade rifles into a pit dug parallel to the grave. It made an extraordinary cloud of smoke. While the grave was still smoking, the earth was drawn back over the body of Sister Gabrielle.

With the twilight began the vigil in the place where Sister Gabrielle had lived. During the vigil the hunters talked about the deceased as if she were still alive. Forty days after the death, in a ritual intended to purify and invigorate the soul of the deceased, the gourd was burned.

Every year, between early March and late May, the brotherhood of hunters organises the *donkun cela*. The *donkun cela*, or 'rites of the crossroads', is the most important ceremony of the brotherhood. During the ceremony, all the members of the brotherhood share a communal meal. At the end of the meal, the *dagas conons* are exhumed. The *dagas conons* are the *kanaris* containing the fried hearts of brave hunters. These hearts are consumed by the brotherhood in secret. It gives them passion and courage.

This is why people say, why everyone says, that the heart of Sister Aminata, colonel of the army of Sierra Leone, served as a delicate and delicious dessert at the end of a merry meal. (A merry meal is a meal during which lots of millet beer is drunk.) *Faforo! Gnamokodé!*

6

As soon as the professional brotherhood of traditional hunters took control of the district around Mile-Thirty-Eight, happiness and us weren't living in the same village any more. (That's the Black Nigger African Native way of saying we weren't happy any more.) We means Yacouba, the crippled crook, the grigriman, the money multiplier, and me, your humble servant, the blameless, fearless street kid. They searched us, stripped us down to our underpants, and took everything we had. When they got down to Yacouba's underpants, instead of just finding his big arse, they found lots of little purses with diamonds and gold in them. Yacouba, the crippled crook, kept his savings underneath his *bubu* in his trousers. When they searched my underpants, they found gold and diamonds too, but it was nothing compared to Yacouba who looked like he had a massive hernia. That's how many purses he had round his waist and in the folds of his trousers. The hunters took everything he had, they took everything we had.

They shut us up in a pen. There were loads of us, soldiers, child-soldiers, women even. There were loads of us, the whole battalion of starving wretches that tag along in the wake of tribal war armies just to get a bit of manioc to eat. They penned us up in a pen where they gave us nothing to eat. We howled with hunger. Yacouba tried to use the fact he was a grigriman, but it didn't wash, it didn't work. Seeing as how we were getting hungrier and hungrier and screaming louder and louder and they couldn't find anything to give us to eat, they let us go. After summary interrogations, they let us go. We were free, with no money and no guns we could use to extort anyone.

The traditional hunters had no need of Yacouba the grigriman; they were grigrimen themselves. I was set free too. The professional brotherhood of traditional hunters, the Kamajors didn't need child-soldiers. Their code forbade them from using children in wars. To fight in a war with them you had to be initiated as a hunter. For the first time, we (Yacouba and me) were confronted with the reality, the uncertainty, of tribal war.

It was only when we were confronted with all this uncertainty that I came to admire Yacouba's resourcefulness for getting by. We left Mile-Thirty-Eight for Freetown. When we got there, he took three tree-trunks and a bit of straw and made a *paillote* ('paillote' means a straw hut). He set himself up in it as a shaman, a grigriman skilled at transforming speeding bullets into water. At first, we had it tough. I was his coadjuter, his assistant. But in the end we had enough manioc to eat. It wasn't a four-star hotel, but at least we had something to eat every day. It was at that point everything happened, proving once again that Allah never sleeps, that he's always watching over the earth, that he's always watching out for miserable needy people like us.

In the end, some kind of truce was reached between the forces of the democrat Tejan Kabbah and those of the four bandit warlords pillaging Sierra Leone. The ECOMOG forces commanded by the Nigerian bandit general, the men of the bandit leader of the Sierra Leonean forces, the forces of the warlord Foday Sankoh, and the forces of the warlord Highan Norman, minister of defence and leader of the Kamajors, the professional brotherhood of traditional hunters. Yes, a balance was reached between all these different freedom fighters, these rival factions, and then the IMF had to go and stick its nose in. The balance of power had been set at eight hundred Kamajors, fifteen thousand soldiers, twenty thousand guerrillas loyal to Foday Sankoh and a surreptitious number of ECOMOG forces. The soldiers in the regular army got a monthly allocation of forty thousand sacks of rice as part of their salary, and one dollar per soldier. The traditional hunters got an allocation of twenty sacks of rice. The IMF found out that the soldiers were eating too much rice and costing the international community too much money. (*Walahé!* Bankers are merciless, they have no heart!) The IMF wanted to scale back the number of soldiers from fifteen thousand to seven thousand and the monthly allocation from forty thousand sacks to thirty thousand. The soldiers grumbled and swore by all their gods that they weren't eating too much. It was just that whenever they tried to wolf down their meagre ration of rice there was always some family member hanging around, right where they were trying to eat. So, on account of African solidarity, the rice had to be shared between an infinite number of people. The IMF hadn't counted on a fucked-up country like Sierra Leone doing African solidarity. The soldiers had the last word, they refused to reduce their forces; they categorically refused to accept less than thirty-four thousand sacks of rice per month.

In order to come up with the extra four thousand sacks of rice and distribute them (the difference between thirty-four thousand and thirty thousand), the poor democratic government of poor Tejan Kabbah was forced to increase the price of fuel across the whole country. But the increase in the price of petrol didn't make much difference. The first month, it paid for three thousand sacks of rice, the second, only two thousand, and the third month, the month of May 1995, there was only money for five hundred sacks of rice. Five hundred sacks. After the officers had been served, the ordinary soldiers, the privates got nothing. The consequences weren't long coming: on May 25, there was a *coup*. It was easier for the coup to take place on May 25 on account of how Tejan Kabbah was guilty of partiality. ('Partiality' means that Kabbah's government was playing favourites with his own tribe, the Mende.)

It started at dawn on May 25, there were bloody clashes between ECOMOG troops and factions in the regular army. The elected president Tejan Kabbah jumped in an ECOMOG helicopter *djona-djona*. The helicopter took him to Conakry, capital of Guinea, to dictator Lansana Conté, where he'd be safe. Once he got there, he had all the time in the world to demand that the members of the CDEAO return him to power. And it was a good thing that he ran away. Because after he'd gone, everyone in Freetown started shooting everyone else. ECOMOG boats from Nigeria were shelling the whole fucking mess. The shelling went on for two days and resulted in the best *coup d'état* – meaning the bloodiest – in the history of Sierra Leone, a fucked-up country that had seen lots of *coups*. More than a hundred dead. After two days massacring, things started to get organised. The new *junta* (a 'junta' means a revolutionary military council) dissolved parliament, suspended the constitution, outlawed party politics, and established a curfew. The *junta* set up the Armed Forces Revolutionary Council government (AFRC).

The putschists ('putschists' means a group of armed people who seize power) ask Johnny Koroma to be leader, to be president. Johnny Koroma accepts. They let him out of prison where they locked him up after the first attempted coup. They appoint Foday Sankoh vice-president and from his cell in Nigeria Foday Sankoh orders his personal guerrillas in the jungle to follow the junta's orders.

Well, as soon as they heard about Vice-President Foday Sankoh, the whole unanimous international community condemned the coup, they came down hard. Everyone was sick and tired of fucking Sierra Leone and its fucking problems.

On May 27, following deliberations, the UN Security

Council, made a statement 'deploring the attempt to over-throw the government and demanding an immediate return to constitutional order'. Important fact: the security council 'calls on all African countries and the international community to abstain from acknowledging the new regime or supporting the authors of the coup in any way whatsoever'.

The thirty-third summit of OUA (Organisation de l'unité Africaine) heads of state took place in Harare, Zimbabwe, from 2 to 4 June. In its final resolution, the summit condemned the May 25 *coup d'état* and demanded that the crisis be resolved under the auspices of the CDEAO

And the CDEAO, well, that's Nigeria. Nigeria meaning the Nigerian dictator, the criminal warlord Sani Abacha. Sani Abacha who, more than anyone else on earth, had had it up to here with fucking Sierra Leone. Sani Abacha who'd been ostracised ('ostracised' means he was ignored) by heads of state after the assassination of representatives of the Ogoni people, an ostracised Sani Abacha who needs to get his virginity back (to find his lost innocence and set out on the right path), Sani Abacha the criminal dictator of Nigeria who wants to take over leadership of the region, Sani Abacha who wants to play the policeman of West Africa. For all these reasons, Sani Abacha sent a whole bunch of warships into the territorial waters of fucked-up Sierra Leone. And the warships shelled the city of Freetown, the martyred capital of this lousy country.

Nigeria and ECOMOG thought this would be a walk in the park, thought it could bring AFRC to its knees in a week, three at the most. That was a mistake. Johnny Koroma and the RUF became a single force of resistance despite the damage and the massive destruction caused by ECOMOG forces.

June 13, Johnny Koroma called on the traditional hunters, the Kamajors. In the name of the mother country, of Sierra Leone, he insisted they bury the hatchet and fight side by side with AFRC against the occupying Nigerian forces. The Kamajors' response, on June 27, was to launch a three-pronged attack on the 38th battalion in Koribundu two hundred miles south-east of Freetown armed with grenades and rocket-launchers. The ferocity of the attack forced the junta to send military reinforcements to Koribundu from Bô and Moyamba. As in Koribundu all the south-east districts became embroiled in these murderous offensives. The formal alliance between AFRC and the RUF against the Nigerians and the Kamajors aggravated the chaos and gave a new base to the RUF, who until that point had been opposed to any compromise. The international community reacted in two ways: intimidation and negotiation.

On the negotiation side, the CDEAO council of foreign affairs in an attempt to implement Security Council resolutions, created a ministerial committee made up of representatives from Nigeria, Côte d'Ivoire, Guinea and Ghana. Representatives of the OUA and the CDEAO were attached to this committee. This Committee of Four was responsible for monitoring developments in Sierra Leone and initiating negotiations with the junta with the aim of restoring constitutional authority in Sierra Leone.

On the intimidation side, they imposed and enforced sanctions. Lungi airport is occupied by Nigerian forces. It serves as a major artillery base constantly bombarding the city. Sierra Leone's territorial waters are rigorously patrolled by Nigerian warships that shell the city at random.

Sierra Leone is starved of everything, of food, of medicines.

The first consequence of the intimidation is a meeting between the CDEAO Committee of Four and a delegate from the junta. This meeting took place on June 17–18 on the twenty-third floor of the Hotel Ivoire in Abidjan. At the end of the meeting, the *communiqué* gives a faint hope that the elected president might get back his armchair as democratically elected boss. Johnny Koroma's representatives show so much good will that the intimidation eases off and bombing scaled back. AFRC representatives are given time to go back home and come back with concrete proposals.

The second round of negotiations in Abidjan opened on 29 and 30 July 1997, back on the twenty-third floor of the Hotel Ivoire. It was supposed to be about the process of re-establishing constitutional order. Surprise! The junta's new proposals are completely in opposition to the points established in the first round of talks on July 17. Now the junta wants to suspend the constitution and stay in power until 2001. The committee expresses its deep disappointment. The negotiators don't allow themselves to be disconcerted by the junta's U-turn. In accordance with the committee's decisions of July 26 at Conakry, the committee suspends negotiations and calls for full sanctions. Ostracised by the international community, the junta is under constant pressure.

From the start of August 1997, Sierra Leone is ravaged by

continuous fighting. It's caught between the bombings of the formidable ECOMOG forces and bullying from the Kamajors. It's destabilised, isolated from the CDEAO. To alleviate internal and external pressures, the junta attempts to relax the vice grip. It requests the help of Guinea in restarting the talks suspended on July 29. The unrepentant dictator Lansana Conté receives a Sierra Leonean delegation at the Petit Palais in Boulbinet on August 9; the delegation is headed by Johnny Koroma's uncle, ex-president Joseph Saïdou Momoh. From the talks, it emerges that the junta is 'disposed to continue negotiations with the Committee of Four mandated by the CDEAO with a view to restoring peace' and loud and clear it says that the date of November 2001 announced for the restoration of civil government is negotiable. It's a question of establishing a timeline for transition.

Round about then, on August 27–28, the twentieth CDEAO summit takes place in Abuja, Nigeria, to discuss the role of ECOMOG in resolving the crisis in Sierra Leone. The summit calls for more sanctions. Nothing but sanctions.

From September 1997, Sierra Leone is starved of food and fuel. It is hit by a dramatic recession which translates as a complete collapse of all economic activity. If the sanctions are disastrous for the economy, the war is just as damaging to sanitation in the country. On top of the shells from Lungi airport occupied by Nigerian forces, strategic points of the capital are bombed causing significant damage. The strict patrolling of territorial waters makes it impossible for boats, trawlers and fishing boats to move.

In response, the professional classes – the civil servants,

the teachers, the doctors and the students – launched a campaign of civil disobedience, triggering government meltdown on top of the economic crisis. There's no anything, no medicines and especially no fuel.

The situation is disastrous, it couldn't be worse than it was. *Walahé!* That meant it was good for us. *Faforo!* Us, Yacouba, the crippled crook, money multiplying grigriman, and me, Birahima, the blameless, fearless street kid, the child-soldier. *Gnamokodé!* We were called up, we took up our duties straight away.

Yacouba, the crippled crook, hopped around on one leg shouting, '*Walahé!* Allah is on our side.' We could go back on duty. Yacouba was appointed grigriman and I went back to being a child-soldier.

The child-soldiers went back to the usual mission, spying. During the spying missions, the hunters killed three child-soldiers. Among the dead child-soldiers there was Siponni the Viper. I've decided to say Siponni's funeral oration because I want to. It was playing truant that did for him, for Siponni. He was in third year of primary in Toulepleu school. He'd already repeated the year twice on account of he didn't go to school much. He played truant after truant, until one day he had it up to here and he jacked it all in and sold everything. Pencil, copybook, slate, all and everything, even his schoolbag. And he bought bananas with his profits. Okay. He did all that in the morning, but then in the evening there was the problem of going home. How could Siponni go home without his schoolbag? He'd get flayed ('flayed' means beaten) by his mother and step-father. He'd get flayed and he wouldn't get any food. No, Siponni couldn't go home. Where could he go? He wandered around and came to a hotel. He saw a big Lebanese guy coming out. He introduced himself to the Lebanese guy as a kid with no maman or dad who was looking for work as a boy. 'No father, no mother, here's a kid I can get to work for free,' the Lebanese guy muttered to himself and hired him straight off.

The next day, Siponni left Toulepleu with his new boss heading for the town of Man. After a couple of weeks working for Feras, his new boss, Siponni noticed that Feras made loads of money and kept it all locked in a wardrobe and never let the key out of his sight. But one night when he was going for a shower, Feras hung up his trousers with the key in them. Siponni took the key, opened the wardrobe, took the briefcase full of money. He went and hid the briefcase in the garden before coming back to say goodbye to his boss. The same night, an old man called Tedjan Touré found him with the briefcase stuffed with cash. Tedjan Touré said he was Siponni's mother's brother, his uncle. Tedjan kept the briefcase and first thing in the morning they took a truck to Danané. There, Siponni stayed with a friend of Tedjan's. Months went by. One day, Tedjan Touré showed up looking heartbroken. After lots of embarrassed explanations he got to the point. The briefcase had been stolen. That's right, stolen. Even with all the looking heartbroken and the long explanations Siponni was still sceptical. Siponni asked a few questions and Tedjan answered them. It was impossible, Siponni didn't believe Tedjan's story and decided he wasn't going to be pushed around. He didn't waste any time, he went straight to the nearest police station to denounce himself as a thief and grassed up Tedjan for receiving stolen goods. The police went looking for Tedjan and brought him to the police station. They tortured him and made him confess. They took both of them (Siponni and Tedjan) to prison. Tedjan to the big prison and Siponni to the kids' prison.

In the children's prison, Siponni met Jacques. Jacques had heard about the child-soldiers in Liberia and Sierra Leone and all he dreamed about was being a child-soldier. He passed on his enthusiasm to Siponni. The two of them decided to go to Liberia, to find the child-soldiers. They waited for a chance to escape, they found it when the prison team went to play against a parish team in a village a few kilometres from Man. Siponni and Jacques took their opportunity and did a runner. They ran deep into the jungle. After much wandering they found the guerrillas. The guerrillas gave them guns and lessons in how to use a kalash. There they were child-soldiers. That's how Siponni got to be a child-soldier.

How did he get the nickname 'the Viper'? For a lot of different things, including the trick he played on Sobresso village. The other child-soldiers were attacking head on. How did Siponni manage, how did he slip past the villagers and get behind them? He cut off their escape. They capitulated, they gave up all resistance and were beaten. Siponni surprised them and betrayed them like a snake, like a true viper.

*   *   *

We fit in well into Johnny Koroma's army. Johnny recruited shitloads of child-soldiers ('shitloads' means lots and lots) because things were getting worse and worse and child-soldiers are good when things are going bad. The child-soldiers were getting crueller and crueller. They had to kill their parents to get initiated. They proved by their parricide that they'd given up everything, that they didn't have any ties on earth, any other home except Johnny Koroma's family. The leaders in Johnny's army were getting crueller and crueller, more and more *bele-bele* (tough). To prove it, they'd eat the hearts of their victims, of victims who fought bravely before they died. They'd point out the cannibal, they were afraid of him, and the cannibal was proud of being thought of as cruel, capable of any inhumanity. ('inhumanity' means barbarism and cruelty.)

We were in Sourougou's troop. Sourougou was a leader in Johnny Koroma's army. We were heading west when — surprise! — we ran into Sekou, our luckless friend, heading east. With Sekou was his own coadjutor, the loyal little Bakary. We broke step with the troop; we took them to one side. Just to get it into your heads, Sekou was a vicious crook, Yacouba's friend. What was Sekou doing in this *kasaya-kasaya?* ('kasaya-kasaya' means country madhouse). Sekou was the marabout who had taught Yacouba the secrets of the grig-riman and money multiplier back in Abidjan. He was the guy who out of the blue ('out of the blue' means suddenly) could pull a white chicken clucking out of the sleeve of his *bubu.*

Yacouba wasn't happy to see him on account of, one, he was competition, and, two, every time he'd seen him, it was always to listen to his troubles. Sekou walked like a guy with a hernia (someone with a big hernia on his *bangala*) on account of having so many, so many bags of gold and diamonds in the folds of his pants. Sekou was just like Yacouba before he got searched by the hunters. Like him, he carried all his savings on him, round his waist and in the folds of his pants. *Faforo!* Looking at him I couldn't help myself, I burst out laughing. He got angry. He didn't let us reel off the miles and miles of greetings that Dioulas, that Mandingos (like they say in pidgin), rattle off when they meet. He said he was surprised to see us heading west. 'All the Dioulas, Malinkés, Mandingos in all of Liberia and all of Sierra Leone are heading east. Why are you going west?' he asked us.

We didn't have time to answer, he told us that something extraordinary had happened in Liberia and Sierra Leone. All the Africans, natives and black savages from both countries, plus the racist American blacks from Liberia, plus the black creoles from Sierra Leone had all ganged up on the Malinkés, the Mandingos. They wanted to chuck them out of Liberia and Sierra Leone, to throw them out and send them back to where they came from. They wanted to boot them all out or massacre the lot of them on account of racism. A Malinké warlord called El Hadji Koroma from Liberia (not to be confused with Johnny Koroma from Sierra Leone) had decided to save the Malinkés. He was gathering them all together in the villages to the east, that's why all the Malinkés were marching east.

Yacouba said he never heard anything about this in Sierra Leone in Johnny Koroma's army. He, Yacouba, was doing fine, was doing very well, thank you, as chief Muslim grigriman, and he was feared and respected by everyone. He hadn't felt the slightest danger and he was going to keep marching west with Sourougou's troop. He didn't believe Sekou's words, he didn't believe them.

Sekou replied that if Yacouba didn't believe, that was his business. But my aunt Mahan believed about the danger of the Black Nigger African Native from all over Liberia and all over Sierra Leone. She'd left with a group of Malinkés heading east to the enclave of El Hadji Koroma. (An 'enclave' is land or territory within the boundaries of another country.)

We were *makou*. (We were really surprised.) That meant, that meant that my aunt was in the east, in Koroma's enclave, El Hadji Koroma. We totally had to save her. We had to desert the army, desert Johnny Koroma's troop. We left Sekou and his coadjutor foot to the road of the damned (condemned to the fires of hell) to the east. We'd join them later; we needed time to duck out (to 'duck out' means to cleverly slip away).

We took advantage of a rest stop to make ourselves scarce, to do a runner. Two days later we headed east, towards the Ivoirian border. We had our kalashes hidden under our *bubus*. That's tribal wars that does that. To make sure it was crystal clear he was a grigriman, a big-shot Muslim grigriman, Yacouba hung loads of grigris round his neck and lots of amulets on his arm. They dangled round his calves. I had a whole lot of amulets hanging from me too and I had a half-open Qur'an in my hand. So much so that all the black savage Liberian natives we met on the way were so scared they got off the road *djona-djona* and stood on the roadside to let us pass.

We walked on like that for three days. On the fourth day, at a fork in the road, we came nose to nose with my cousin Saydou Touré. The cousin was extravagantly armed. At least six kalashes, two hanging round his neck, two hanging from each shoulder, and ammunition belts wrapped all round him, and chains of grigris on top of the ammunition belts. He had a beard and his hair was tousled ('tousled' means in a mess). Even though he looked all disgusting, I threw my arms round his neck, I was so happy to see him.

After we hugged, I looked the cousin up and down, down and up, curiously. He stared at me and with a scary laugh he said, 'In a *kasaya-kasaya* country like Liberia, you need at least six kalashes to deter people ('deter' means to discourage someone from action). My cousin Saydou Touré was the biggest brawler, the biggest liar, the biggest drinker in all the north-west of Côte d'Ivoire. He drank so much, he fought so much, that he was forever on trial, forever in prison, he was never out of prison more than one month in six. My other cousin, Doctor Mamadou Doumbia, had taken advantage of one of cousin Saydou's rare periods of freedom to send him on a perilous mission. In desperation (as a last resort) he asked him to go and find his mother, my aunt Mahan, in fucked-up Liberia over there. He would give him a million CFA francs if he could find her. Saydou gladly accepted. Aunt Mahan was the poor woman we'd been looking for ourselves for more than three years all over tribal war Liberia. We were happy to see cousin Saydou. We decided to all go together.

Cousin Saydou Touré was a storyteller (a storyteller is someone who substitutes invented stories for real life), a liar. He loved Doctor Mamadou Doumbia, who often sent him money when he was in prison. He talked about him all the time with lots of tenderness, with friendship and love.

When he was seven, little Mamadou Doumbia had walked eighty kilometres with an old freedwoman and a little girl. Back then, Black Nigger African Natives were still stupid. They didn't know anything from anything: they gave food and lodging to any strangers who showed up in their village. And Mamadou and his two friends were given food and shelter on the house ('on the house' means for free) the whole ten days of their journey.

They arrived in Boundiali one night and the two women sat down and explained the reason for their mission. Allah had bestowed on the village a huge brood of brats, ('a brood of brats' means a lot of noisy children) born to the savage hunter. The savage hunter was the little brother of the head of the Touré family. The savage hunter had decided to give his older brother a share of his brood, the patriarch's share of the hunter's offspring. Mamadou was that share. They had come here with little Mamadou to give him to Touré, Touré the patriarch. Uncle Touré had the power of life and death over little Mamadou. Little Mamadou would sleep wherever his uncle told him to sleep, without complaining. Uncle Touré, the patriarch, thanked the women who brought him, took Mamadou by the arm, hailed his first wife, and gave little Mamadou to her. Little Mamadou would belong to her. The patriarch's first wife was called Tania and Tania was Saydou's mother.

The school year had already started. The patriarch brought his nephew to the white colonial *toubab* colonist commander. The commander authorised little Mamadou to be enrolled in the school at Boundiali.

Saydou and little Mamadou went to school together. Saydou was the same age as Mamadou and Saydou was jealous: he didn't want his mother to look after little Mamadou with all the tenderness she gave him. Saydou's maman kept them apart and she always blamed Saydou for everything.

They slept, Saydou and Mamadou, on a mat by the feet of mother Tania. And little Mamadou always peed the bed. He wasn't clean; he was disgusting. Big maggots ('maggots' means fly larvae) crawled all over the mat. Saydou thought up an idea to get rid of little Mamadou. One night, he did a pooh, a big pooh, on the mat at the end of the bed and in the morning he mulishly ('mulishly' means obstinately, stubbornly, without budging an inch) swore that it wasn't him, Saydou, who had relieved himself, but little Mamadou. Seeing as little Mamadou was a chicken, a coward, he didn't know how to defend himself. He sat down and cried; that was proof, proof that he had done the pooh. Saydou's mum, Tania, got angry. As punishment, she sent little Mamadou to sleep in the boys' hut with the boys (the servants). The boys put him on his own at the back of the hut. He still peed the bed and still lived surrounded by wriggling maggots. The maggots that swarm under the mats of filthy little brats.

Saydou and Mamadou still went to school together; Mamadou turned out to be clever, really clever, and Saydou was a dunce. Saydou had all sorts of problems. He couldn't pronounce things, his writing was a spidery scrawl. In a developed country, Saydou would have been sent to a psychologist. When he was ten, the teacher had no choice but to expel Saydou from the village school.

For four years, during the last war, Mamadou went to the village school by himself. But there was no teacher. After the war, Mamadou was too tall, too old to be in primary school. He was expelled too.

The village teacher tutored Mamadou for the school certificate, which he passed. This was considered an achievement by Black African Third-World Natives with no initiative. An achievement that the commander and administrator of the white sector decided to encourage. They made legal changes to Mamadou's birth certificate. Now little Mamadou was five years younger and therefore fulfilled all the necessary conditions for admission to primary school in Bingerville. He went to the primary school and then to normal school in Gorée and then after to medical school in Dakar.

While Mamadou was pursuing his brilliant education, Saydou was starting out on his cursed life. Fight after fight, prison after prison, escape after escape. Escaping across Côte d'Ivoire, across French West Africa. Wandering in the Sahara – Nigerian Sahara, Tibesti Sahara, Libyan Sahara. Back home to his village, where it was prison after prison again, until the last time he was released and Mamadou asked him to go into the Liberian jungle to rescue his mother.

Saydou told the story of his cursed life and the life of the doctor Mamadou Doumbia all the way on our journey through tribal war Liberia. For three days and three nights. On the fourth day, we reached the village of Worosso, not far from the Ivoirian border. We means Yacouba, the money multiplier, Muslim grigriman, Saydou, the bandit sent by Doctor Mamadou to rescue the aunt, and me, the blameless, fearless street kid, the child-soldier. Worosso was where El Hadji Koroma's camp was. The compound there had human skulls on stakes all round the boundary like all the tribal war camps in Liberia and Sierra Leone. *Walahé!* That's tribal wars. We walked through something that looked like a gate, marked out with two skulls on stakes with two armed child-soldiers between them. We got our Malinké greetings ready. Suddenly we were surrounded by about ten guerrillas armed to the teeth. They'd been lying on the floor of the forest round the camp. They'd promptly got to their feet. We still wanted to do the greetings. Without listening, they shouted, 'Hands up!' Without hesitating, we put up our hands. They disarmed us. Searched us down to our underpants. That's tribal wars that's responsible for that kind of welcome. Still not responding to our greeting, they told us all to explain ourselves.

Saydou went first. Saydou told unbelievable stories about his exploits. First he'd been a colonel in ULIMO. That was a lie: he'd come straight as an arrow from prison in Boundiali. It's on account of being a colonel, he said, that he had six kalashes. That was a lie too. When Doctor Mamadou had sent him to rescue his mother, Saydou wanted to take guns. Doctor Mamadou Doumbia had gone with him to Man, to the Liberian border where you can get kalashes at bargain prices. The doctor wanted to buy him one, Saydou wanted six. Mamadou bought him six, thinking he might be able to use them to trade, as financing for his adventures ('financing' means support during a journey). And it was armed with six kalashes that he headed into the tribal war Liberian jungle. Saydou kept on making up stories. He pretended he was happy, really happy, when he found out that El Hadji had retreated with all the Malinkés to create a safe haven for the Malinké people ('safe haven' means sanctuary provided by some authority). He was so happy he'd decided to leave ULIMO. On account of his rank and his bravery, ULIMO didn't want to let him go. The ULIMO leaders had begged him to stay with them. He said no and he publicly accused his ULIMO bosses of having killed loads of Malinkés themselves. The ULIMO bosses weren't too happy. They set a trap for Saydou, then arrested him, disarmed him, chained him, and put him in prison. This was still Saydou telling his adventures. The ULIMO bosses didn't realise that no one on earth could keep him, Saydou, locked up. Saydou smashed the walls of the prison and stood in front of them, arms dangling, his chains vanished. Well, at that point the ULIMO bosses and the ULIMO soldiers and everyone at ULIMO started shooting him: they fired at him but it was useless. The bullets transformed into water and ran off his body. The ULIMO bosses and the soldiers and the child-soldiers panicked. They all bolted, they ran away leaving their guns behind. Saydou picked up six and that was the ones he was bringing to El Hadji Koroma.

After Saydou, Yacouba explained himself. Yacouba started making up stories too. He'd been a lieutenant-colonel in the army of Johnny Koroma in Sierra Leone, lieutenant-colonel grigriman. It was a lie, a barefaced lie. He said he was made lieutenant-colonel on account of his amazing *grigris*. He'd rendered the shelling from the warships and ECOMOG planes inoperative. All the shells from the planes and all the warships out at sea and all the cannons at the airport fired on Sierra Leone turned into water. ECOMOG forces fired shells at the people of Sierra Leone for nothing, the shells never exploded. Yacouba had managed to bewitch a whole army, an army and all its weapons of war. And that's not all. He'd managed to make all of Johnny Koroma's guerrillas, all his soldiers and child-soldiers, invisible to the ECOMOG invaders. The invaders were firing at thin air.

Yacouba was told to stand down. Now it was my turn.

Listening to the big guns, Saydou and Yacouba, lying like chicken thieves, I wanted to sell myself too. I said that I was a commander too, a commander in Johnny Koroma's child-soldiers. I was a champion spy. I'd managed to infiltrate right into ECOMOG headquarters. I'd managed to nick their maps, all their maps. So that ECOMOG were bombing in the dark (meaning at random). I'd put laxatives into the chief of staff's whisky and he got the shits. He couldn't stand still. Using a dugout, I'd rowed out to the ships in territorial waters that were shelling. I got on board the ships and poisoned the marines' rations. The marines dropped like flies. They thought it was an epidemic. The marines deserted the ships. That's why the shelling had stopped.

After all our stories, the guerrillas started answering our Malinké greetings. They wished us welcome. From the way we talked, they knew we were Malinké and not Gios or

Krahns come to spy. So we could make ourselves at home, we were welcome in Worosso, in El Hadji Koroma's camp. We were patriots. We would be incorporated into El Hadji Koroma's army with the same rank that we had in our previous units. The great patriotic army of generalissimo El Hadji Koroma needed officers of our calibre.

That's how we all got to be senior officers in El Hadji Koroma's army. We all had it easy: we were all entitled to batmen (a batman is an orderly) and, even better, double rations of food.

But you didn't get to eat well in El Hadji Koroma's army. All you got was a little handful of rice in a corner of the plate that wasn't enough for a sick grandmother on her last legs with nothing to do except lie in her hut and die all the time. There wasn't enough rice. Absolutely not even nearly enough.

El Hadji Koroma's system was based on exploiting refugees, ripping off NGOs. The troops – meaning us – captured Malinké refugees the NGOs were required to feed. And we insisted the NGOs route everything that was supposed to go to the refugees through us. We generously helped ourselves before thinking about the people it was intended for. Every time an NGO showed up with food or medicines, the poor well-trained refugees would stand at the gate and deliver the same speech.

'Why will you not trust our brothers, the men of El Hadji Koroma who have saved our lives? Everything you give to them, they give to us. They are our brothers. When they receive something, it is as though it were placed in our own hands. We cannot come out to accept your donations and you cannot come into the camp. We, the refugees of Worosso camp, refuse all donations which do not come through our brothers.'

Faced with the misery, the destitution of the refugees and their determination, the NGOs gave in. And we helped ourselves before thinking about the refugees.

We played this game every day for three months. But we had not forgotten the aunt. No. We were still actively looking for her, but on the sly. We means Colonel Saydou the liar, Lieutenant-Colonel grigriman Yacouba, the crippled crook, and me, Commander Birahima, the blameless, fearless street kid. We were searching on the sly because if anyone there found out that we were there looking for the aunt, we'd lose our stripes.

One day, Saydou came and told us something incredible. At first Yacouba and me thought it was another one of his stories. But he took me by the arm and brought me to the generalissimo's house. It was true, really true, Doctor Mamadou Doumbia was here in Worosso in El Hadji Koroma's camp. Really here. The doctor had walked in and talked to El Hadji Koroma himself. The generalissimo had given his orders. Investigations were made. Aunt Mahan was tracked down. She had arrived at the camp ill. Probably she had malaria and a raging fever that meant she was confined to her mat (bed). Back then, the Malinkés in the camp, all the Malinkés, were boycotting the NGOs (deliberate severing of all relations with an organisation). They didn't want to work with the NGOs because the head of the NGOs refused to work with their saviour, El Hadji Koroma. NGO stretcher-bearers would come to the camp to evacuate the sick to a field hospital. Aunt Mahan refused. She completely refused so as to show solidarity with all the refugees in the camp. For three days she lay there, and on the fourth day she died like a dog. May Allah have mercy on her.

Led by the generalissimo's aide-de-camp, we went to the hut where my aunt had been. My aunt's last words were for me. She was really worried about what would happen to me, according to one of the refugees from Togobala who had been with her in her dying moments. I cried my heart out, Colonel Saydou crumpled on the ground. Yacouba said prayers and said that Allah hadn't wanted me to see my aunt again; may Allah's will be done on earth as it is in heaven. When I saw Saydou collapse and beat the ground with his two hands, I was sick to my stomach and I wiped away my tears. Because Saydou was crying and saying, 'My aunt's death makes me sad, very sad, now I cannot bring her to the doctor and the doctor will not give me my million CFA francs.' It was the million Saydou was crying for, not my aunt.

The refugee from Togobala who was with my aunt in her dying moments was called Sidiki. Sidiki gave the doctor the tattered *pagne* and blouse the aunt had been wearing. The doctor kissed them. *Faforo!* It was pitiful to see.

Sidiki had the effects of another refugee from Togobala who also died observing the rules of the boycott. He was an interpreter. His name was Varrassouba Diabaté. He was a Malinké and, among the Malinké, when someone is called

Diabaté that means he is from the *griot* caste; *griot* from father to son and he's not allowed to marry a woman who isn't *griot*. Varrassouba Diabaté like everyone from his caste was intelligent. He could understand and speak lots of languages: French, English, pidgin, Krahn, Gio, and other Black Nigger African Native savage languages from fucked-up Liberia. That's why he had a job as an interpreter at the HCR (High Commissioner for Refugees). Varrassouba had lots of dictionaries: *Harrap's Larousse, Petit Robert*, the *Glossary of French Lexical Particularities in Black Africa*, and other dictionaries of Black Nigger African Native savage languages from Liberia. Every time a big someone from the HCR wanted to visit Liberia, they sent Varrassouba Diabaté along with him. One day, Varrassouba Diabaté accompanied a big somebody to Sanniquellie in gold-mining territory. He met the gold bosses. He knew the bosses of the gold mines made loads of money. Varrassouba Diabaté ditched the person he was supposed to accompany. He stayed in Sanniquellie and set himself up as a bossman. He was making loads of money when the Krahns arrived in Sanniquellie. They didn't want Malinkés being bossman gold miners. Varrassouba got the fuck out *djona-djona*. He arrived in El Hadji Koroma's camp, the Malinké refugee camp with all his dictionaries. He intended to go back to Abidjan, to his well paid job as an interpreter. Unfortunately, he was too sick when he got to the camp. On account of the boycott, he couldn't get healed. He died and they threw his body into a mass grave. Sidiki didn't know what to do with the dictionaries. He offered them all to me. I took the *Larousse* and the *Petit Robert* for French; the *Glossary of French Lexical Particularities in Black Africa*; the *Harrap's* for pidgin. That's the dictionaries I've been using for my bullshit story.

Still following the *aide-de-camp*, we headed to the mass grave where the aunt's body had been dumped. We bowed down by the grave to pray. The prayers were led by Yacouba, but Yacouba hadn't finished saying the first '*Allahu Akbar, Allahu Akbar*' when Sekou showed up, no one knew from where. And he piously crouched down. Sekou is Yacouba's friend, the friend who could make white chickens appear out of the blue. Sekou was a grigriman and a money multiplier like Yacouba. The prayers were said by Yacouba in a voice so pure and clear that they went straight up to heaven. But maybe they weren't accepted because out of the seven people around the mass grave where the aunt was buried, three of us were criminals. The seven people were: the doctor, the generalissimo's aide-de-camp, Yacouba, Sekou, Saydou, Sekou's coadjutor, and me, Birahima, the blameless, fearless street kid. The three criminals who feared neither God nor man on account of who Allah couldn't accept the prayers were Saydou, Yacouba and Sekou. That's why we had to say more prayers, more *suras*, lots more prayers for the repose of my aunt's soul.

Now the road was straight, the road to Abidjan via Man was straight. There were five of us in Doctor Mamadou's four-by-four Pajero. The doctor, his driver, Yacouba, Sekou and me. Saydou hadn't come along, he didn't want to come. At the last minute, he took his courage in both hands and asked the doctor a question.

'Mahan was one of my aunts so I should have looked for her free, gratis, for nothing. But all the same you promised me a million CFA francs. And I got used to having the million and all the time I was travelling I could see myself as a millionaire. I was going to set up a grocer's shop with that million. Now the aunt is dead, tell me, tell me straight, are you going to give me any of the million?'

'Not a centime, nothing at all, because I have my mother's funeral to organise,' replied the doctor.

So Saydou turned away and said, 'I'm staying here in Worosso so I can make the most of my rank as colonel.'

I was sitting in the back of the four-by-four, squeezed between Yacouba and Sekou. The big-time criminals were very happy. The folds of their trousers were heavy with purses full of gold and diamonds and the doctor had promised to help them in Boundiali so they could get their birth certificates changed. They could get new identity cards so they could openly practise their trade as money multipliers in Abidjan. *Walahé!*

I was flicking through the dictionaries that I'd just inherited. Namely, the *Larousse* and the *Petit Robert*, the *Glossary of French Lexical Particularities in Black Africa* and *Harrap's*. That's when this brilliant idea popped into my calabash (my head) to write down my adventures from A to Z. To recount them with clever French words from *toubab*, colonial, racist, colonising French and big Black Nigger African Native words, and bastard nigger pidgin words. It was at that moment that my cousin, the doctor, said to me, 'Tell me everything, little

Birahima, tell me everything you've seen and done; tell me how all this happened.'

I got good and comfortable, good and settled, and I started: The full, final and completely complete title of my bullshit story is: *Allah is not obliged to be fair about all the things he does here on earth.* I went on telling my stories for a couple of days.

First off, Number one . . . My name is Birahima and I'm a little nigger. Not 'cos I'm black and I'm a kid. I'm a little nigger because I can't talk French for shit. That's how things are. You might be a grown-up, or old, you might be Arab, or Chinese, or white, or Russian – or even American – if you talk bad French, it's called *parler petit nègre* – little nigger talking – so that makes you a little nigger too. That's the rules of French for you.

Number two . . . I didn't get very far at school; I gave up in my third year in primary school. I chucked it because everyone says . . . etc., etc.

Faforo! Gnamokodé!